HIGHLAND TREACHERY

Elizabeth Penney

Annie's®

AnniesFiction.com

Library of Congress-in-Publication Data
Highland Treachery / by Elizabeth Penney
p. cm.
I. Title
2015952133

AnniesFiction.com
(800) 282-6643
Secrets of the Quilt™
Series Creator: Shari Lohner
Series Editors: Shari Lohner, Janice Tate, and Ken Tate
Cover Illustrator: Jonathan Bouw

10 11 12 13 14 | Printed in China | 9 8 7 6 5 4 3 2

1

Cabot Falls, Vermont
Present Day

"I was surprised to learn I have a Scottish ancestor." Sofia Parker sat on the edge of the reading chair in her bedroom and carefully opened the ancient leather journal she had inherited. "But the diary confirms it."

"That red-and-black plaid is definitely a Scottish tartan." Julie tossed her curly red hair.

Sofia's two closest friends, Julie Butler and Marla Dixon, were examining the heirloom quilt Sofia's Italian grandmother had passed on to her. It was a vibrant, colorful patchwork pieced together from materials collected over centuries and hidden away in a carved wooden Renaissance-era *cassone* along with the diary. Ever since Sofia had received her unexpected legacy, her friends had been helping her discover the stories behind the squares in the quilt.

Sofia paused and took a breath before reading. Every time she translated a new entry in the ancient journal, she felt a shiver of anticipation. The quilt and the diary were like a portal to her family's history, which so far had proven to be captivating, rich with dramatic events and fascinating people. "That swatch once belonged to Isabelle Caroline Ripa who lived in Edinburgh in 1745."

Marla leafed through a guide to tartans that Sofia had asked her to bring from the Cabot Falls Public Library where Marla was head librarian. "In 1746 the English government banned the wearing of the plaid."

Sofia and Julie exchanged glances. "Tartans were banned?" Sofia asked. "I didn't know that."

"They certainly wear them today," Julie said. "A friend from college hired a bagpiper for her wedding, and he wore a kilt." She smiled at the memory. "He looked great, but I couldn't stand the noise that bag of wind made."

"The bagpipe isn't for everyone," Sofia agreed. *Had Isabelle enjoyed it?*

Marla picked up another book and quickly searched the pages. "Here it is. Tartans were outlawed for almost forty years. After the Jacobite Uprising in 1745, any man or boy wearing a tartan was jailed or transported to the West Indies for seven years."

"Jacobite Uprising. That sounds familiar." Sofia set the diary aside and picked up a piece of paper. Since the diary was in Italian, she translated each entry using an English-Italian dictionary supplemented by computer translation software and her own spotty knowledge of the language. "I've only done a few sentences so far, but Nonna's diary said that Isabelle was the daughter of an Italian court musician and a Scottish noblewoman whose family was loyal to the Jacobite cause."

"What was—?" Julie began.

Marla interrupted, her blue eyes glowing as she swung into a lecture. She loved nothing more than sharing knowledge. "The Jacobites supported Bonnie Prince Charlie's claim to the throne of England. In 1745, he returned from exile in France to stage a rebellion from Scotland." She shrugged slim shoulders. "It was unsuccessful, of course, and that's what led to the ban."

"I wonder if my ancestor was involved with the uprising." Sofia's gaze went back to the tartan square. "Maybe someone wore it during a battle, someone Isabelle knew and loved."

"Was the tartan in the book, Marla?" Julie asked. "We can start with that for a clue."

"That's right," Sofia said. "Doesn't every family, or clan, have their own?"

"They do," Marla said, "but what can complicate it is that there are many branches with different surnames in each clan." She stopped at a page in the tartan book and carried it toward the bed where she glanced back and forth between the page and the quilt. "Your tartan looks like the MacGregor Red and Black. Worn by the famous Rob Roy MacGregor, immortalized in the book by Sir Walter Scott."

Julie snapped her fingers. "*Rob Roy*, right? Didn't they make a movie of that too?"

Marla crossed the room and handed the book to Sofia. "Yes. And we have both at the library."

"I vote for watching the movie," Julie said. "It's easier than reading those old classic novels."

"Oh, Sir Walter Scott's prose style isn't that bad," Marla said. "Without him, many Scottish stories and legends would have been lost."

Sofia looked up from the entry about the MacGregor tartan. "Thanks for bringing these books over, Marla. I have a feeling I'm going to be leaning on you heavily to help with research."

Marla laughed as she stacked the other books neatly on the dresser. "Anytime. You know that. It's what we librarians live for." Her eyes widened. "That reminds me. We received a flyer about a Highland Games event in Creighton, Vermont, the week after next. Dr. Benjamin Campbell, a clan expert, is going to be there. Maybe he can help us with information about the MacGregors."

"Highland Games. Those sound great." Julie pulled out her phone and began to search the Internet. "Here it is. A celebration of Scottish and Celtic culture. Athletic competitions, sheepherding, music, dancing, traditional crafts, and food."

The website played a fragment of bagpipe music, and the eerie sound sent chills down Sofia's spine. *Scottish culture is part of my history. And I can't wait to explore it.*

Margaret's reserve lasted until the tenth bottle. "All right, I'll tell you. There's a ball tonight at Holyrood Palace." She sighed deeply, pressing a hand to her generous bosom. "The thought of dancing with Bonnie Prince Charlie makes me swoon."

The young sovereign was only twenty-four, and Isabelle confessed a quickening of her own pulse at the thought of seeing him again. While entering the city on horseback, he displayed a stately grace in his fine tartan coat and red breeches, a white rosette pinned to the velvet cap adorning his handsome head. The crowd of twenty thousand cheered wildly to welcome their new king.

"I haven't seen an invitation." Feeling a pang of disappointment, Isabelle filled the last bottle.

Margaret waved a dismissive hand. "Of course you're invited. For one thing, your father is playing in the orchestra tonight. And anyone in the MacDonald clan is welcome. We've been staunch Jacobites since . . . since forever." History wasn't Margaret's strong suit.

But Isabelle knew she was right. Her mother's ancestors had supported King James II, deposed in 1688 in favor of his own daughter, Mary, who had ruled with her husband, William. The Jacobite movement had gone underground then, surfacing periodically as hopes were pinned on one descendant after another.

Someone knocked on the workshop door. "Yes?" Isabelle called.

Nan, the maid, opened the door. "A gentleman customer for ye, milady."

"Show him in." Isabelle quickly corked the bottles, wiped them, and set them on the shelf next to other potions, all identified with handwritten labels affixed to the bottles.

The broad-shouldered young man who entered wore a belted plaid of red and black tartan over a linen shirt, hose on his muscled legs, and a blue bonnet perched on his loose brown hair. He bowed, sweeping the hat from his head. "Rory MacGregor, at your service,

Lady Isabelle. I wish to purchase liniment for Lord Ogilvy." He cast his eyes toward Margaret, who batted her lashes and smiled.

Isabelle shot her a quelling look—*How inappropriate to flirt with a servant!*—and asked him a few questions about the lord's symptoms. After a moment's thought, she made a selection from her tins of salve. "This is my best ointment, excellent for severe rheumatism such as Lord Ogilvy endures. But I caution you, apply it no more than twice a day."

The man stared at the small round tin in the palm of his hand, puzzled. "Why is that?"

"It contains wolfsbane, which is safe only in very small doses. A large dose might be fatal."

"I'll be sure to tell Lord Ogilvy." Looking uneasy, he slid the salve into his pocket and dug out a coin for the purchase. With a tip of his hat and an extra smile for them, he left, footsteps banging on the stairs.

"Well," Margaret said with relish, "do all your customers look like that?"

Ignoring her, Isabelle put the coin in her cashbox, then straightened her shelves, making a mental note to mix up more of the salve. Like the cough syrup, it was popular during damp, bone-chilling Scottish winters.

"Are you finished in here now, I hope?" Margaret asked, tapping her foot, arms crossed, like an impatient governess. "We need to prepare ourselves for the ball."

The window revealed a slice of bright blue afternoon sky above the six-story building opposite. "Why, it is barely three. We have hours yet."

Margaret grunted in exasperation. "How often do you get to dine with a monarch? We must look our absolute best. Besides, the palace will be swarming with handsome Highlanders. Such a change from our pale, puny Edinburgh men."

Isabelle raised a brow. "Like Lord Ogilvy's man? Be careful, Margaret. Don't let those uncivilized warriors turn your head."

Later that evening, while riding down the Royal Mile in the carriage to Holyrood Palace, Isabelle had to admit she shared Margaret's interest in the visitors. The cobblestone street was thronged with soldiers, most of whom were dressed in Highland regalia, many with legs swinging bare under kilts despite the chilly night. They meandered in and out of shops and taverns while others gathered on street corners to talk. The local merchants were certainly making the most of the occasion, some even using barkers to tempt customers to buy.

Margaret was wide-eyed, craning her neck to stare at each new sight. "They say Prince Charles lacks support, but you'd never know it," Margaret said. "It appears every man in Scotland is here."

"Father said they're coming in by the hour from every corner of the Highlands." Isabelle took a deep breath, feeling excitement and a sense of national pride tingle in her veins. The Stuart line had originated in Scotland and was now poised to rule again. A victory for the Highlanders would be especially sweet after crushing defeats during the last Jacobite rising three decades before. Her maternal grandfather had played a major role in that conflict and by some miracle retained his fortune and standing afterward.

As the carriage rolled to a stop in front of Holyrood Palace's main entrance, which was tucked between stone towers, Margaret patted her powdered curls. "How do I look?"

Isabelle checked her cousin's appearance, from her high-piled hair to rouged cheeks to the lace-trimmed décolletage on her pale green silk gown. "Incredibly lovely," she replied honestly. "How about me?" She sat up straight, wincing against the bite of her stays, and tugged her elbow-length sleeves into place.

"Perfectly gorgeous," Margaret said. "I love red on you with your dark hair." She grimaced. "If red hair was in style, I wouldn't have to powder mine so thickly." She sneezed, as if underscoring her words, and wiped her nose with a dainty lace handkerchief. "See what I mean?"

Isabelle laughed. "Yes. Let me out before I start." She slid across the leather seat toward the door.

Margaret held up her hand. "Wait. I almost forgot something." She rummaged in her brocade reticule and pulled out two rosettes of white muslin—the Jacobite cockade. "Margaret Murray, wife of the prince's secretary, insists that we all wear these as a sign of loyalty and unity." She gestured for Isabelle to lean closer and pinned the cockade on her left shoulder. "Now do mine." She handed Isabelle the second rosette and a pin.

One of the guards helped them out of the carriage while another opened the massive entrance door and waited patiently as they fluffed their wide skirts into place. Stepping aside to allow Margaret to enter first, Isabelle glanced up at the royal arms of Scotland over the door and the motto *Nemo me impune lacesset* carved into the lintel. "No one harms me with impunity."

Let it be so for our bonnie prince.

Inside the palace, they ascended the wide grand staircase side by side, footsteps muffled on the carpet. A candle lantern hung on a chain, its flickering light casting shadows on the magnificent plasterwork decorating the ceiling. The ornate floral pattern reminded Isabelle of icing on a cake.

Margaret stopped dead on the landing, her breath coming in pants. "Are your stays too tight?" Isabelle whispered, casting a glance at the guard below. No one else was in sight, but she could hear strains of music and the hubbub of voices drifting from upstairs.

Her cousin's cheeks were stark white under the rouge. She flapped a hand in front of her face. "I'm frightened."

This was an unusual admission from Margaret, known for her saucy high spirits. Isabelle reached out and took her hand. It was clammy. "We know almost everyone. And the others don't matter."

"The prince matters." Margaret's eyes were so wide, white showed all around the irises.

Isabelle wished she had thought to give Margaret some calming chamomile tea before they left the house. However, her cousin succumbing to a fit of nerves was the last thing she had expected. She racked her brain for something to say. Then inspiration struck. She leaned closer and whispered, "The prince is a man like any other. He puts his breeches on one leg at a time."

"Unless he is wearing a kilt." Margaret's smile was sly, and to Isabelle's relief, she began to climb the stairs again.

The roar of sound in the great dining chamber was deafening, chatter and laughter threaded with music from the small string orchestra valiantly sawing away in the corner. Isabelle's eyes went to her father, who sat with his cello cradled between his knees, head bent over its massive belly as he skillfully plied his bow. Sebastian Ripa was a composer and founding member of the Musical Society of Edinburgh. She wondered how he felt about playing for the Jacobites since he'd always been careful about hiding his political views.

Margaret grabbed her elbow. "Where should we sit?" She tipped her chin, searching the crowded tables for seats. The most distinguished Edinburgh nobles and men of the prince's court were seated at a dais up front. The center chair, taller than the rest, remained conspicuously empty, along with a few others.

"Over there." Isabelle pointed to two chairs. "Next to Brenda

Morrison and Allan Fraser." Blond and full-figured with a hearty, laughter-filled approach to life, Brenda was one of their closest friends.

"Squeeze over, squeeze over." Brenda motioned for Allan, resplendent in tartan and lace like the other men present, to make room for her friends. The women's hooped petticoats took up almost as much room as two men, so they required a good deal of space.

Once they were settled, Brenda laced her fingers with Allan's. "You know Allan is an artist, right? Well, he has the job of engraving banknote plates for the prince." She cast a fond glance at the slightly built blond man. "He also designed the fans they're giving us tonight as mementos."

"You are the prince's official artist, then?" Margaret's eyes were wide. "How fortunate."

Allan shrugged, a rueful smile flitting across his handsome features. "It was a condition of our betrothal."

"Betrothal?" Margaret squealed with joy and clapped her hands. "How delightful!"

Isabelle, sitting closest, gave Brenda a hug and a wink. "Imagine that. You two will soon be husband and wife." Brenda had confided months before that she planned to reel in the wealthy and well-connected Allan.

Brenda laughed. "Yes, I told this rogue I wouldn't marry him until he pledged to support Prince Charles." She nudged Isabelle with an elbow. "I couldn't let our side down and marry a Whig."

Isabelle suppressed a smile. Not only had her friend landed her choice of groom, but she had also managed to convert him politically.

With a flourish of notes, the orchestra reached a crescendo and fell silent. A moment later, bagpipes wailed in the doorway. The guests scrambled to their feet with a scrape of chairs. The prince had arrived, elegant in red velvet breeches and jacket with trimmings of blue and white brocade, a blue satin sash slung across his chest.

Margaret gasped as she painfully clutched Isabelle's arm. "Isn't His Majesty handsome?" She wasn't the only one crying out. Many women—young and old—were swooning with excitement at the arrival of their hero. With an effort, Isabelle quashed her own girlish response, not wanting to behave in a way that was unseemly.

He is indeed magnificent. Would they be as enamored of his quest if he was short and squat?

The crowd continued to cheer as Charles proceeded to his spot on the dais. After his men moved to their places, he gave a wave to indicate that everyone should sit down.

He remained standing. "I, Charles, Prince of Wales, Duke of Rothesay, Regent of the Kingdoms of England, Scotland, France, Ireland, and the dominions thereunto belonging, offer greetings unto all His Majesty's subjects." He went on to detail the glory of coming out of exile to take his rightful place as king, and he commended all his loyal followers for their assistance.

Many toasts and speeches followed this rousing address, during which servants brought out tureens of cock-a-leekie soup followed by platters of beef collops and friar's chicken. Mindful of her corset, Isabelle ate sparingly of the traditional dishes, more interested in watching the crowd's antics. Somber businessmen known for their rectitude were jumping to their feet to proclaim oaths to the prince's campaign in loud, passionate voices. A bearded Highlander recited a poem in a Gaelic dialect many could not understand, judging by the puzzled faces, but all were moved by the fervor of his conviction. Even the women were raising their cups with "Hear, hear!" at every toast.

As the meal wore on and the excitement in the room grew to fever pitch, the men at the head table forgot their dignity and joined in. Last to speak was Lord Lochmere, a dour dumpling of a man who had lived in exile with the prince and was considered one of his closest and most powerful advisers. Like many nobles in the inner circle, he took rooms at Holyrood.

The nobleman raised a hand to greet and quiet the crowd. A long pause followed. Then his gaze became fixed and he began to gently sway back and forth.

"The man must be in his cups," Brenda murmured. "For shame."

But then Lochmere clutched his chest with both hands, gasping and gurgling like a fish out of water, his face turning gray. Isabelle jumped to her feet. *Doesn't anyone understand? The man can't breathe!*

3

Cabot Falls, Vermont
Present Day

"Look," Mom," Matthew called.

Sofia paused in watering the daylily bed and turned to see her ten-year-old son holding a big rock with both hands over his head. With a grunt, he flung the rock, which landed a scant three feet away from where he stood.

Luke, at the advanced age of twelve, laughed. "That was lame. I bet I can do better." He ambled forward and bent to pick up the rock.

"Be careful. Don't hurt yourself." Sofia tugged on the hose so she could move along to the next bed, this one holding pink coneflowers and spiky purple astilbe.

Luke's face turned red as he held his breath in preparation for throwing the heavy stone. "Ugh!" The rock landed with a thud a little farther than Matthew's attempt. "We're practicing for the Highland Games."

Sofia's husband, Jim, came around the corner of the house in time to hear Luke's explanation. "Actually, they only use one hand in the stone put." He settled himself in a lawn chair near Sofia. "And I don't think they have that event for kids your age anyway."

"Are you sure?" Luke scowled. "I'm practically a teenager."

"Positive. But there are others you can sign up for. Like the caber toss and the haggis hurl."

"Haggis?" Matthew bent over, hands to his belly as he laughed. "What is that?"

"Sheep stomach." Although Jim's voice was matter-of-fact, Sofia noticed the twinkle in his blue eyes.

As Matthew went into new gales of giggles, Luke collapsed onto the grass, a comical look of disgust on his face. "Are you serious?"

"Sure am. If you're lucky, they freeze it first." He shot a smile at Sofia, who suppressed her own giggle. "By the way, I found us a cabin to rent for the week. It's on a small pond, so we can swim and fish when we're not at the games."

Finished watering, Sofia released the sprayer and tugged the hose back to its base. "That sounds great. We'll make a real vacation of it."

Jim's silver Honda Civic pulled into the drive and their daughters, Vanessa and Wynter, got out with a slam of car doors. "What's going on?" Vanessa asked as she and her sister joined the others in the backyard.

"Your dad found us a cabin so we can stay there during the Highland Games in Creighton," Sofia said.

"Cool." Vanessa, eighteen, slid a smile toward her fifteen-year-old sister. "Guys in kilts." She tugged on her denim shirt to demonstrate.

Wynter's blue eyes widened as she clapped a hand over her mouth. "Really?" Her gaze was speculative as she looked at her father and brothers. "Are you guys going to wear kilts?"

"Heck no," Jim said.

"What are kilts?" Matthew asked.

"Skirts for boys," was Luke's prompt reply. His brother screeched and ran around the yard.

The girls plopped to the grass as Sofia finished winding the hose and took the chair next to Jim. "I suppose you could wear a kilt," Sofia said, "since my family has Scottish blood and you're in my clan now."

Jim's lips quirked. "I think there's Scottish blood on my side too. My mother was a Gregg."

"Really, Dad?" Wynter's face lit up. "I've always wanted to join a clan." She was currently going through a phase of obsession with Scotland-themed television shows, movies, and books.

"Which clan are the Greggs?" Vanessa asked.

"We'll have a chance to find out at the games," Sofia said. "I'm going to see what we can learn about my ancestor, and we can ask about your dad's family too."

Vanessa nudged Wynter with an elbow. "We can choose the tartan we like best, Mom's or Dad's."

Wynter pulled a piece of paper and a pencil out of her pocket and began to sketch something. She showed the picture to Vanessa, who laughed.

"Luke. Come see the kilt Wynter drew for you."

"No way." Luke jumped to his feet, poised to escape. "What's for dinner, Mom? I'm starving."

Sofia judged the slant of the afternoon sun across the treetops. "You're right, it is almost dinnertime. How about firing up the grill, Jim? We can have burgers and fresh corn on the cob from the farmers market."

Matthew circled closer, panting from running around the yard. "I want a burger. No sheep stomach for me, Mom. Yech."

"Sheep stomach?" Vanessa's eyes were wide.

"Don't ask," Sofia said as she slid out of the lawn chair with a sigh. "Girls, come help me put dinner together, please."

After dinner, the children went for an evening bike ride with Jim while Sofia took the opportunity to brew a cup of tea and go online for a few quiet moments. She loved the long Vermont summer days and how they allowed her active family to spend more time outside getting fresh air.

Four growing children cooped up in our small house is a sure recipe for cabin fever. Thank goodness for warm weather. She took a sip of tea and then clicked onto the Highland Games website, eager to learn more about the activities offered.

Dr. Campbell was slated to lecture on clan heritage as well as hold appointments to speak privately with those researching their histories. She signed up for one of the few slots left in his schedule, afraid to wait until they went to the fair in case he was all booked up. She hoped she would have enough time to find out about the MacGregors and the Greggs. And she still needed to find out about Isabelle's Scottish mother, so there might be a third clan to learn about.

Reaching for a pen in the desk drawer, she jotted a note for Jim to get additional information from his mother about her ancestors. Marla would help her research Isabelle, she was sure. They might as well go as prepared as possible so as not to waste the professor's precious time.

After submitting her appointment request, Sofia clicked on the page with the overall schedule, one she could download and print. A banner at the bottom caught her eye.

"Shortbread Bake-Off Sponsored by Best Biscuits."

Besides drawing and painting, Sofia loved nothing better than baking. In fact, her dream was to start an artisan bakery business.

She quickly scanned the rest of the text. "Do you have a shortbread recipe that uses the finest Vermont butter and offers a new twist to a traditional favorite?"

No, but I could invent one in a jiffy.

"Open to professional cooks only. Best Biscuits will license the winner's recipe for national distribution. Entrants must prepare biscuits on-site in licensed trucks. To enter, please call . . ."

Best Biscuits was a top company with a large line of packaged cookies and cakes. Sofia often bought their products when she didn't have time to make homemade cookies. A contract with them might pay a lot, money her family could certainly use. *Four growing children also mean growing bills. And I don't even want to think about college.*

Professional cooks only. She baked and catered for public events and private parties and had been paid, so she hoped that put her in the professional category. She glanced at the clock. It was probably too late to reach someone, but she could call and leave a message, at least.

She grabbed her cell phone and punched in the numbers. To her surprise, someone picked up almost immediately, a woman with a gravelly voice. "Highland Games office. Sylvia speaking."

Sofia introduced herself. "Thanks for answering. I wasn't sure there'd be anyone there this late."

Sylvia gave a huge sigh. "I'll be working until midnight every night until this shindig is over. So, how can I help you?"

"I was calling about the shortbread contest to find out if you're still taking entries."

Another huge sigh from Sylvia. Sofia braced herself for bad news. "Actually, we do have one opening. We . . . lost an entrant. She was a great cook too. Probably would have won."

Sofia's heart leapt. Maybe that meant she had a chance. "I'm sorry to hear that, but I'd like to take her place."

"All righty, then. Let me get you in the system."

Sofia listened to the sounds of clicking on a keyboard.

"Good thing you called tonight. The slot would probably have been gone by tomorrow."

"And a good thing for me that you answered." Excitement flooded Sofia at the news that she'd gotten in under the wire.

"That's quite a contest Best Biscuits is putting on," Sylvia continued. "I wish I could cook. But my shortbread comes out like a hockey puck, although a hockey puck might taste better."

"It's a great contest." Not only was it a golden opportunity, but it would give her something to do while at the games. Throwing rocks—or haggis—and doing jigs wasn't exactly her thing.

"Name?" Sylvia led her through the form. At the end, she added, "Now, you'll need to bring a food truck because all cooking has to happen on-site."

"Oh yeah. I read that. I thought maybe you provided the trucks." Sofia's shoulders slumped. Where was she going to find a truck on such short notice? They weren't exactly common.

"No, we don't supply . . . but hey, I have a thought. Maybe you could rent Madelaine Abbot's. Well, the one she was going to use. I'm sure the company would rather not have it empty when they could be collecting rent."

"That sounds like a solution. What do I need to do?"

Sylvia gave her the owner's contact information. "I'd call Russ right away, tonight if possible. Before he pulls it off the fairgrounds."

"Do you have any idea how much Russ charges?" She should have thought of that before agreeing.

"No idea," was Sylvia's breezy response. "But I do know you can make a lot of dough with one of those trucks." She gave a throaty chuckle at her own pun.

"I can sell baked goods during the fair?" That would be perfect. Even if she didn't win the contest, she could still walk away with a profit from the week.

"I hope you do, if they're as good as Madelaine's." Sylvia tut-tutted. "Who would have thought someone her age would die of a heart attack?"

"How old was she?" Sofia whispered, shocked at this news.

"Forty on her next birthday. Such a tragedy. She dropped dead right outside the food truck, face-first in the grass."

The double door silently shut behind Sofia as she entered the marble-floored main lobby of the Cabot Falls Library. Marla was standing behind the horseshoe desk, using her sleek new computer to help a patron check out. Sofia was jarred by the contrast between the updated equipment and the Victorian building's carved woodwork, ornate tin ceiling, and stained glass windows. But she was glad to note the old library still smelled the same, an evocative blend of old and new paper, worn leather, and lemon furniture polish.

Marla said goodbye to the woman and then turned her attention to Sofia. "What brings you here?" she asked with a wide smile. "More books on Scotland?"

"Sort of." Sofia set her tote on the floor and pulled out a notebook. "I need recipes. I'm going to enter a shortbread contest at the Highland Games."

"Shortbread?" Marla's fingers were already flying over the keys. "You didn't have any recipes in your cookbooks at home?"

"There were a couple of basic ones. But I'm trying to be as authentic as possible, so I was hoping to find something direct from Scotland."

"Hang on. I'll see what's available."

Sofia glanced around the library while she waited for Marla to search the files. On such a beautiful summer day, very few people were in the reading room or at the long tables in the reference department. Her family had gone swimming at a nearby lake, but she'd wanted to look for recipes for the contest and for other baked items to sell.

"Wait until you see this." Marla sent a file to the printer. "I've found something really marvelous. *The Cook and Housewife's Manual,* first printed in 1826."

"You'll let me take out such an old book?"

"It's a reprint." She slid the page across the desk. "Tell me about this contest."

Sofia filled her in without mentioning Madelaine, still shivering inside at the idea of taking a dead woman's place. But as Jim had said more than once, Sofia dropping out wouldn't change what had happened to Madelaine.

"So, you're going to be in a national contest and make money while you're researching your ancestor. That's fantastic." Marla turned to her assistant. "Bonnie, can you please watch the desk? I'm going out on the floor for a minute."

In the stacks, Marla quickly found the right section and pulled books off the shelves. "Here's *The Cook and Housewife's Manual.* And you should make scones." Marla handed her a second book. "And tarts." Another. "And don't forget bread." A fourth volume, this one quite thick.

"That's enough," Sofia said with a laugh. "I'll probably only make about four or five different things to sell."

Marla shrugged. "It's always good to start with too much information and then winnow it down." She slid a finger along the titles, searching for any last must-haves. "I think you have the best ones there."

"Thanks," Sofia said, doing her best to hang on to the slippery book jackets as she followed Marla through the stacks. "You've certainly given me plenty to work with."

At the desk, Sofia plopped the books down as Marla nipped around to her station. "I want to research Isabelle's mother," Sofia said as she dug out her library card, "but the diary doesn't say anything about her, except that she was a noblewoman. Do you know anyone who can help me with records in Edinburgh?"

Marla scanned the card, then slid the first book across. "The state library has a genealogy expert. I'll email her and see what she can do."

"Hello, Sofia," a soft voice said at her elbow.

Sofia turned to see her elderly neighbor, Pat Cooper, her arms full of books. "Hi, Pat. How are you?"

Pat set her tall stack down on the counter. "I'm fine. Picking up a little light summer reading."

Sofia and Marla chuckled at her joke, although Sofia suspected Marla heard that one a lot.

Adjusting her eyeglasses, Pat peered at the books Marla was checking out for Sofia. "Doing some baking?"

"Yes, I've entered a shortbread contest at the Creighton Highland Games. If I win, my recipe will go national."

"That sounds like a wonderful opportunity." Pat tapped her lips with a finger, her characteristic action when thinking. "I know of one baker over that way. Sandy Wallace. She owns Wallace Treats on the village green in Creighton." She patted Sofia on the arm. "Sandy's the one to watch, my dear. Her shortbread melts in your mouth, as I recall."

Sofia gave a little laugh. "Thanks for the warning." She picked up the cookbooks and slid them into her tote. She hoped she'd be able to devise a recipe good enough to best her rival. *Too bad it's only a few days until the games begin.*

4

Edinburgh, Scotland
September 1745

Isabelle darted through the maze of tables to where Lochmere had collapsed. Behind her, the diners burst into chatter and laughter, believing the man was inebriated. Heedless of her fine gown, she knelt on the flagstones beside him and put her fingers to his throat. His pulse was very faint and slow, yet his brow shone with sweat.

"Can you hear me, Lord Lochmere?" she asked into his ear.

His eyes flickered open, the irises already dull. "I'm cold . . . so cold." He could barely move his lips and jaw, which made his words almost unintelligible.

"Move away, move away," an imperious voice said above her head.

Isabelle glanced up to see the prominent Edinburgh physician, Dr. Donaldson, glaring down at her. She had crossed swords with him more than once concerning the best course of treatment for a patient.

"Lord Lochmere is not drunk, sir. He is ill."

"I will be the judge of that." He made a shooing motion.

Isabelle reluctantly rose to her feet and stepped aside to give the man room, watching closely as he assessed the patient's symptoms.

"What is your diagnosis, milady?" a deep voice said close to her ear.

Turning, she was startled to see Rory MacGregor, the customer at her shop earlier that day. *Where did he come from?* No servants were dining in this hall.

Then his presence triggered a terrible thought. Lochmere's symptoms were similar to those of a fatal dose of wolfsbane absorbed through the skin: the chest pain, the sweating, the stiffness of the lips, a sensation of cold. *How could that be?* Rory had told her he was buying the salve for Lord Ogilvy, hadn't he?

She shook her head to buy time. "I have my theories on the matter, but Dr. Donaldson is in charge here, not I."

Rory glanced at the good doctor as Donaldson rose to his feet, puzzlement on his narrow face. Rory sidled closer to Isabelle, lowering his voice as he spoke behind his hand. "I wager you are the better healer." His tone was sly, almost intimate.

She jerked away, offended at this impertinent familiarity from one lowborn. "You flatter me." She raised her voice. "What do you think, Dr. Donaldson?"

The doctor shot her a glare and then called out, "This man is suffering from a paroxysm of the heart."

Bonnie Prince Charlie jumped up from his seat, dismay etched across his handsome features. Lochmere was one of his most loyal supporters. "What can we do, Doctor?"

"We must move quickly. I need several strong men to carry him to his chamber."

The crowd was somber now as two of the biggest and strongest men rose from their seats with a scraping of chairs. Rory joined the others, crouching down to help them move the stricken man to the blanket someone found. The prince remained seated, but the rest of the nobles clustered around to watch. Isabelle worked her way around the circle until she was beside Lord Ogilvy, who had been seated next to Lochmere at the head table.

"Dreadful turn of events, is it not, milord?" She gave him a smile that she hoped conveyed both admiration for his lordship and concern for the suffering man. Ogilvy wasn't a large man—he stood barely taller than Isabelle herself—and his calves in their hose were spindly and weak. But he wore the authority of his noble birth in the tilt of his beaked nose.

As she'd hoped, the middle-aged Ogilvy responded politely. "It certainly is. Just moments ago the man was eating and drinking most heartily. He was speaking of how much he enjoyed eating good plain Scottish cooking after years of rich French food." He cocked his head. "I know your reputation as a healer, Lady Isabelle. Could it be a humor of the digestive system? Perhaps our national dishes no longer agree with him."

The men had the patient securely situated on the makeshift stretcher and were now preparing to lift him. "One, two, three," Rory called. "Lift."

"It is more than indigestion," she said. "He is having difficulty breathing." The men were now carting Lochmere away, Rory in the lead, moving carefully through the tables to the door.

The intelligence in Ogilvy's hooded gaze warned her that anyone who took him to be a foppish and vain aristocrat would be making a deadly mistake. "Despite the balls and feasts, we're living in dangerous times, milady. Remember that."

Before she could respond, Ogilvy bowed and moved away, joining another nobleman nearby. *What on earth did he mean? Did he suspect that Lochmere's illness was an attempt on his life? Or merely that the stress and strain of war had caused his sudden illness?*

On an impulse, Isabelle followed the band conveying Lochmere out of the dining hall, heedless of the curious glances thrown her way. She had barely exited when chatter and laughter broke out again, the lord's distress apparently causing only a momentary disruption in the festivities.

The small band wove their way through large empty public rooms to another, smaller staircase. With grunts and groans and cries of "Easy, now!" and "Watch his head!" they carried the ailing man up to the next floor, which was poorly lit by torches and dismally damp. These chambers hadn't been used in decades, as evidenced by the cobwebs draped in corners and thick dust on every surface. Isabelle could even see their footsteps on the flagstones, darker smudges in the gray.

But inside Lochmere's room, it was clean, and a merry fire burned in the grate, dispelling most of the chill. The men carried him to the canopied bed and transferred him to it as gently as possible. Dr. Donaldson moved to the bedside to check Lochmere's pulse.

"How is he?" Isabelle asked, moving forward out of the shadows.

One of the other men jumped, giving a startled laugh. "I didn't see you standing there, lass," he said. "I thought I might be seeing a wee ghostie."

"Lady Isabelle is a healer." At Rory's words, the other men gave her nods of respect.

She threw him a quick smile of thanks for his support. "How is he, doctor?" she asked again, raising her voice.

Dr. Donaldson kept his eyes on the patient, the irritated movement of his head the only sign he heard her. Dropping Lochmere's wrist, he laid a hand on his chest.

"Is the man going to live?" Rory spoke loudly, exaggerated impatience in every word.

Isabelle suppressed a smile. Rory MacGregor was a bold one, all right.

The physician shook his head, his expression a picture of dour pessimism. "I doubt it. His heart rate is slowing."

Braving Donaldson's disapproval, Isabelle moved to stand beside the doctor. Lochmere's face was ashen, and his chest barely moved with each labored breath. She reached out and touched his hand. His flesh was icy cold, further confirmation that poisoning was probably the cause of his distress.

Her eyes darted around the area nearby. What could he have ingested to cause this reaction? In addition to a half-burned candle and a tinderbox, the bedside stand held a mug with dregs of some beverage and a small missal, the type of thing a gentleman might keep in his chest pocket to read during a quiet moment. A pair of tortoiseshell spectacles lay folded on the book, an intimate and touching reminder of the man's humanity. She could picture him tucked up in bed, reading something edifying before going to sleep.

"Make yourself useful and spark that candle." Donaldson's voice was a growl. "A man need not die in the dark."

More out of sympathy for Lochmere than a desire to obey the physician, Isabelle picked up the tinderbox, struck a flame, and lit the candle. As its wavering light illuminated the area, she saw something shining on the floor between the bedside table and the bed.

Using the toe of her slipper, she pulled it out farther. It was a small silver tin, identical to the ones she used for wolfsbane salve. She narrowed her eyes and squinted. Yes, that was her label on the lid, the *W* and *B* written in large letters to warn users to take care.

A thunderous knock sounded at the door. Isabelle jumped, shock tingling through her limbs. *Is the guard here to arrest me for poisoning Lord Lochmere?* Would anyone believe it was inadvertent—an accident, in fact?

At Donaldson's directive, Rory strode across the room to answer the door. Her pulse thundered in panic as she glanced around wildly. Her first irrational thought was to hide herself behind the window curtains or in the wardrobe. Then she noticed a door to an adjoining room. Could she—?

"His Excellency to see Lord Lochmere," a guard announced to the room. He stood aside to let Prince Charles enter the room. Several courtiers followed, all wearing suitable expressions of concern as they peered at the man lying in the bed.

At the sight of the prince, Isabelle released the breath she didn't even know she had been holding, her knees sagging in relief. No one knew about the salve. How could they? He wasn't even her patient. The very idea that she would be seized and arrested was all in her very fertile imagination. Maybe she was wrong about the diagnosis too, and his illness was indeed a paroxysm of the heart. She had merely leapt to conclusions.

"How is he, Dr. Donaldson?" Prince Charles asked, his brow furrowed in concern. He approached the bed but stopped a few feet away, politely allowing Lochmere some room.

Hands clasped behind his back, Donaldson strolled to the prince's side, his lips pursed dolefully. "It is only a matter of hours, Your Excellency, if not minutes. Nothing to be done in a case like this, I am afraid."

Prince Charles, a devout Catholic, crossed himself. "It was his time, then. Let God's will be done." His courtiers copied him, as did the men attending.

Seeing that everyone's attention was on the monarch, Isabelle ducked quickly and grabbed the tin. Hiding it in her palm, she slid it through a slit in her gown to the muslin pocket worn underneath.

Rory glanced her way, and she gave him a coquettish smile. Let him think what he would; she owed him no explanation.

"Send for the priest," Prince Charles said to one of his men. "At least that way he can receive the last rites." He crossed himself again. "May angels speed him to his rest." He turned to the others standing by. "Please, go join the festivities. The ball will be starting any moment."

"You are not canceling the event then, Your Excellency?" Dr. Donaldson asked in surprise. Lochmere was one of the prince's closest advisers, after all.

Prince Charles shook his head. "It would cast a pall over the celebration, which the good people of Edinburgh have attended in force." Determination hardened his young, handsome features. "We cannot afford to lose the momentum created by their support." In a lower voice he added, "And in wartime, many a life is lost. Unfortunately, that is the price of a righteous cause. At least this tragic passing is due to natural causes."

When Donaldson didn't answer, the prince sent him a sharp glance. "That is your diagnosis, doctor? Natural causes?"

"What was that?" The doctor seemed startled, having apparently been lost in thought. "Yes, that is correct. Natural causes." His tone of voice didn't quite match the certainty of his words. He sounded vague, almost doubtful.

Watching this exchange closely, Isabelle wondered what the doctor was thinking. He'd seemed adamant that Lochmere's heart had failed. Did he suspect another cause now? Or worse, was he involved somehow in an attempt on Lochmere's life?

She pushed these deranged thoughts away. The most likely scenario was that Lochmere had gotten hold of the salve and applied too much. But putting forth this theory would only bring trouble.

For all Isabelle knew, she had pocketed an old tin of wolfsbane, the last bit finished days ago, wholly unrelated to the failure of Lochmere's heart. Still, the little container lay like a lead weight against her thigh.

No one must ever know of its existence.

The door opened again and a black-robed priest slipped in. Priests were a rare sight in Scotland since the Protestant Reformation. But Charles, raised in Rome, was a devout Catholic. This cleric must have accompanied him from France.

Isabelle moved to the fireplace to make room for the priest. He pulled out a vial of oil, anointed Lochmere on the head, and began to pray in a language Isabelle recognized as Latin. A deep silence fell upon the room, all attention on the stricken man. Isabelle shuddered. The fire's warmth and gentle crackle was the only comfort against the cold weight of death.

As the priest uttered his final amen, Lochmere gave one last gasping exhalation. He was dead.

5

Cabot Falls, Vermont
Present Day

"What's going on, Mom?" Luke asked as he barged into the kitchen, followed by Matthew. Both boys were sweaty and dirty from kicking a soccer ball around the backyard.

Sofia opened the oven door and pulled out a slightly overdone tray of cookies. "I'm experimenting with recipes for the shortbread contest."

"Goody." Luke moved closer to peer at the tray. "Ugh. Those look burned."

"Yeah, they sure do." Matthew nodded vigorously. His hand snaked out and grabbed a rectangular cookie from one of the plates on the table that were piled high with various concoctions Sofia was testing. Before Sofia could stop him, he crammed it into his mouth. Mid-chew, he stopped and frowned, then grabbed a napkin and spit into it. He ran for the sink, filled a glass with water, and drank.

"I guess the caraway seeds are a no," Sofia said wryly, setting the pan down on the stove. So was the ultrathin basic recipe. "Crispy" wasn't the word for what had happened to that batch.

"What was wrong with it?" Luke asked Matthew after he finished gulping down the entire glass of water.

"Tasted like cabbage," Matthew said.

"Good guess," Sofia said. "There's no cabbage in it, but I use that same spice in cabbage dishes."

"I don't like it in cabbage either," Matthew said, wiping his mouth with his forearm and leaving a streak of mud across his face.

"Can I try a different one?" Luke's hand hovered over a pile of fluted circles.

"Not now. I was planning to have a tasting after dinner." She surveyed the half-dozen plates of shortbread ruefully. Hopefully one of them would be a winner, at least here at home.

"Knock-knock." Pat Cooper was at the back door, peering through the screen. Sofia had left the door open to release some of the kitchen's heat.

"Come on in," Sofia said, stripping off her oven mitts. She turned to the boys. "Go get washed up."

They skedaddled as Pat entered the kitchen holding a small paper bag in one hand. She glanced around at the dirty mixing bowls, ingredients lined up on the counter, and plates of finished cookies. "You've been busy."

Sofia went to the refrigerator. "Can I get you a glass of iced tea? I was about to pour myself one."

"Sure." After locating the only empty spot on the table and setting down her bag, Pat sat at the table. "Did you find a good recipe yet?"

Sofia placed a frosty glass in front of Pat and took a seat at the end of the table. "Not yet." She waved a hand at the cookies. "I made six batches this afternoon and the word is in on two so far. Thumbs down."

Pat took a sip of tea and smacked her lips in satisfaction. "Don't lose faith yet, my dear. Shortbread is pretty simple. Flour, butter, and sugar? How can that go wrong?"

"Very easily, like piecrust." Sofia shook her head. "Mixing the dough is one thing. Then there's chilling the dough—or not—before you roll it out. Too thin and it burns. Too thick and it's like a wad in your mouth."

"What if I gave you a foolproof and delicious recipe?" Pat's eyes behind her glasses were sly. "Would you be interested?"

"Of course. Why didn't you say something earlier?" *Like before I wasted three pounds of expensive Vermont butter?* she added silently.

Pat picked up the bag and unrolled the top noisily. "I wasn't sure I still had this." She extracted a recipe card from the bag with gnarled fingers and handed it to Sofia. "That was my grandmother's. She got it off a cornstarch box."

"Cornstarch?" Sofia was skeptical as she studied the card. The other ingredients were powdered sugar, flour, and butter.

"I know. It sounds terrible, but it's actually very flaky and tender. Give it a try."

Why not? She'd add Pat's recipe to the taste test roster and not tell anyone what it contained.

Pat was rummaging around in her bag again. She placed a round ceramic object in front of Sofia. "I thought this might make the cookies look very attractive."

It was a cookie stamp with a Scottie dog motif. Sofia picked it up and thought about how the shortbread would look. She'd been thinking about a traditional plain rectangular or circular shape. But why not use the dog? It would be eye-catching at least.

"What's that?" Wynter had wandered into the kitchen and spotted the cookie stamp.

Sofia handed it to her. "It's to decorate the shortbread."

"Oh, it's so cute. Promise me you'll use it." She handed it back to Sofia.

"I will. Can you tell your sister it's almost time to set the table?" To offset the rich cookies for the evening tasting, she'd prepared a chef salad for dinner.

"That sounds like my cue," Pat said, draining her glass. She pushed back from the table. "Let me know how the cookies turn out."

"Why don't you come by tonight and find out?" Sofia suggested. "We're doing a tasting at seven."

That evening was the regular meeting of the Pinot Painters—Sofia, Julie, and Marla's painting group. Instead, her friends left their art supplies at home and came over to taste shortbread along with Pat and her husband, Homer.

"I'm glad I listened to you and ate a light supper," Marla said. She examined a round cookie before taking a bite. "What did you say this one was?"

"Lemon." Julie pointed to the hand-lettered signs Wynter had placed in front of the plates covering the dining room table.

"This tastes bad, Mom." Matthew handed Sofia half a cookie. At least he wasn't spitting them out anymore. It was a Margaret Dods's early-1800s recipe, which called for candied fruit and almonds. It was enjoyed by the adults but not the children, she noticed.

Former professor Homer Cooper devoured six cookies, reminiscing the whole time about his trip to Scotland, where he had enjoyed high tea at four every afternoon. "A wee bit of clotted cream would be a fine touch," he said, putting on a fake Scottish accent.

"This one is perfect," Jim said, grabbing another one off the cornstarch plate and tossing the whole thing into his mouth. "It dissolves in your mouth."

Pat smiled at Sofia. "I told you so," she whispered under her breath.

"It's my favorite too," Luke said. With a furtive glance at his mother, he swiped two, one for each hand.

Jim cocked his head. "There's something extra in it. I can't quite identify the taste."

"I'm keeping it a secret." Sofia had added vanilla to give the flavor a boost.

Finally, all the votes were in and judged by the number of cookies left on the plates. Pat's vintage recipe as amended by Sofia won hands down, and the Scottie dog decoration was also a favorite.

Now all she needed to do was impress the judges at the contest.

A few days later, Sofia and Jim loaded up the Suburban with luggage, cooking supplies, and kids and drove over to their cabin on Akers Pond near Creighton. Sofia hadn't driven that way very often, right into the heart of the Green Mountains, a landscape characterized by abrupt peaks and steep meadows dotted with cows.

"This part of Vermont reminds me of Scotland," Sofia said. "Maybe that's why they have the Highland Games here."

Vanessa leaned forward from the backseat, cell phone in hand. "Listen to this, Mom. Vermont has one of the highest percentages of Scottish Americans in the country."

"I'm sure immigrants liked settling in places that reminded them of home," Jim said. "They don't call it New England for nothing."

"Look up Italians," Wynter said. Sofia's Italian heritage was important to her and she had passed that same interest on to her children.

"At least she's using that phone as a reference tool," Sofia whispered to Jim. Although she was worried about the teenage obsession with cell phones, she and Jim had agreed that once Vanessa started driving, she needed one for emergencies. Frankly, Sofia couldn't imagine not being able to contact her daughter whenever she wanted, especially at night or in bad weather.

Although the games didn't start until the next day, the small, quaint town of Creighton was already crowded with automobiles and visitors. Brick storefronts and white frame buildings festive with window boxes and bright awnings lined Main Street. Sofia spotted Wallace Treats on one corner. The bakery's hours were painted on the glass, announcing it was open from 6 a.m. to 2 p.m. She glanced at the dash clock. Ten after two. She'd missed the chance for a covert reconnaissance of her competition's baking ability.

After Jim stopped at the rental agency to pick up the cabin key, they continued through downtown. The buildings gradually gave way to countryside, and they soon passed the entrance to the fairground where the Highland Games were to be held. Right after, Jim turned onto a side road that wound through fields and woods, the blue flash of Akers Pond visible through the trees. One pretty farm they passed had extensive flower gardens and sheep gazing in the pastures. Bluebell Farm, a sign read.

That looks idyllic.

Sofia loved Cabot Falls, but the idea of living on one of the many small farms in Vermont intrigued her. A waterfront house was a close second, and the first sight of the A-frame log cabin they were renting thrilled her.

"This is great, Jim," Sofia said when he pulled to a stop near the front steps. The kids burst out of the car. The girls ran up onto the porch, the boys down to the pond.

Jim pulled out the keys and opened the car door. "Yeah, we were lucky. Someone canceled. I'm sure everything around here is booked up solid."

Inside, the cabin was simple but spacious. One big room

served as living room, kitchen, and dining room. There were two small bedrooms beyond and a loft upstairs. Sofia parked her duffel in the loft and then perched on the queen-size bed to enjoy the view of pine trees framing the pond through the floor-to-ceiling front window. *I'd hate to have the chore of washing that window.*

While she would have liked nothing more than to relax for the rest of the afternoon, she had to go over to the fairgrounds and check on the food truck. Assuming that it might not be ready for use, she'd brought cleaning supplies along. With a sigh, she got up and stretched. Jim and the children were already fishing on the dock. She wouldn't ask them to come with her and spoil their fun, but she would put Jim in charge of dinner. If they didn't catch any fish, then they could eat hot dogs. The boys actually preferred them.

At the fairgrounds, she followed signs to the office, a low-frame building near the huge livestock barns. Over at the barns, men and women were busy unloading sheep and horses, no doubt for the sheepdog trials starting the next morning. With animals boarded on-site, many owners stayed in travel trailers or motorhomes parked neatly behind the barns. A short distance away, activity was brisk on the midway with people bustling around the white tents, wooden booths, and food trucks. The smell of frying potatoes and meat drifted on the air, mingled with less pleasant odors of diesel fuel and animal droppings.

Inside the office, a thin, middle-aged woman with a short gray bob stood behind a counter, phone to her ear. By her gravelly voice, Sofia assumed she was Sylvia, the woman she'd spoken to on the phone.

While she waited for Sylvia to get off the phone, Sofia busied herself pulling out the application form, insurance information, and the special food service license she had been required to obtain. Then she mentally ran down her list of tasks. Once the truck was clean to her satisfaction, she would unload the cooking supplies and ingredients she'd brought from Cabot Falls. In addition to the shortbread, she'd decided to make lemon tarts, cranberry scones, raisin bars, and honey oatcakes. Not being sure of how much she would sell, she had a hard time estimating the amount of ingredients she'd need. They could always run to the local grocery store to restock. Although that would cut into the profits, at least she wouldn't have a lot of waste.

"Can I help you, hon?" Sylvia asked after she hung up the phone.

Sofia placed the paperwork on the countertop, along with a check for the vendor fee. "I'm Sofia Parker. Russ said you'd have the key to the food truck."

"Hold on." Sylvia held up a hand. "We'll get to that in a minute." She pursed her lips, peering through her spectacles as she ran a finger over each line on the forms, checking to be sure everything was filled in correctly.

Sofia shifted from foot to foot impatiently. Behind her, others drifted in.

The older woman slid the license back to her. "Post that in the food truck where it's visible. We keep the application." She processed the check, stapled the insurance information to the application, and filed it in a long box on the table behind the counter. Then she slowly, methodically located another packet of papers and placed them in front of Sofia along with a key attached to a green plastic tag.

By this time, Sofia was ready to scream. As she reached for the key, Sylvia put her hand on top of it. "Hang on. We need to go over our food service rules."

"Please do." Sofia bit back her irritation. Something told her it was better to stay on Sylvia's good side.

Indeed, Sylvia went through every item on the checklist, from cleanliness to food safety rules. Most of them were old hat to Sofia, but she managed to keep quiet and nod. Behind her, the others in line shifted and muttered impatiently. When Sylvia finally handed the packet over, Sofia thought she might wilt with gratitude.

"I'm all set, then?" Sofia shoved the papers into her tote. She could organize them later at the truck. She took the key and put that in her purse.

"Don't you want to go over the contest rules?" Sylvia broke her gaze and fixed her eyes on someone behind Sofia.

Sofia turned to see a tall woman pushing through the line. Her first impression was of a queen thrusting aside the serfs, an image reinforced by the woman's erect posture and haughty expression. Her close-cropped pale curls and almost colorless eyelashes and brows only served to heighten the impact of her glacial blue eyes.

"Sylvia. I don't have water at the truck yet. What's the problem?"

The older woman ducked her head, avoiding eye contact. "I'm sorry, Sandy. I'll call Harvey on the radio and find out what's going on." She turned and grabbed a walkie-talkie off its stand. Before talking into it, she sent Sofia a sly smile. "Sandy Wallace, meet your shortbread contest competition. She's taking Madelaine Abbot's place."

Sandy whirled around, glaring, and Sofia had the distinct feeling she had been thrown under the bus. Someone in the line snickered.

"Who are you?" Sandy's tone was demanding as she took a step toward Sofia and loomed over her.

Sofia realized Sandy was the owner of Wallace Treats, the baker Pat Cooper had said to watch. *What a way to meet a fellow competitor!* Sofia moved her legs apart slightly to take a firmer stance. She held out her hand. "Sofia Parker. From Cabot Falls."

Sandy ignored her hand, her eyes narrowing to piercing slits. "Are you a professional baker? I've never heard of you."

Dropping her hand, Sofia tried to laugh it off. "I'm not surprised. I mostly do catering."

The other woman gave a rude shrug of one shoulder and turned away. "Well, good luck." She put her not-so-pert nose in the air. "You'll need it."

Sofia picked up her tote but then hesitated. She didn't want to give the bakery owner the satisfaction of thinking she intimidated her. "People's taste buds won't care if they've heard of me," she said, straightening her shoulders. "And good luck to you too."

"Attagirl," someone in the crowd muttered.

Without waiting to see Sandy's reaction, she strode toward the door. The others waiting gave her covert smiles as she pushed by.

Outside, she took a deep breath and tried to still her racing heart. It appeared she had made an enemy.

6

Edinburgh, Scotland
September 1745

"He is gone, Your Majesty. God rest his soul." With a bow to Prince Charles, the priest swept from the room as silently as he had entered.

Charles slowly approached the bed, an expression of intense sorrow on his face. He stared down at Lochmere's waxen features. "Godspeed, dear friend." He bent and gave Lochmere a kiss on the cheek.

Are those tears in his eyes? Feeling as though she was intruding on a private moment, Isabelle turned and stared into the flames, resting her palms on the mantel.

Behind her, she heard Charles speaking with the doctor. "Make the necessary arrangements, if you would, Donaldson. In our situation, we must make haste, unfortunately." Isabelle assumed he meant that in a time of war, there would be no state funeral as would normally occur for a man of Lochmere's stature.

"As you wish, Your Excellency. I will post a servant to keep watch tonight."

Isabelle said a silent prayer for Lochmere's soul before leaving the room in company with the others. The last thing she wanted to do was to return to the ball, but to do otherwise would only arouse questions she didn't want to fend off. Having never met Lochmere before tonight, she could scarcely claim grief.

Rory came alongside her as she scurried down the hallway

toward the staircase. “A sad affair, was it not?”

She kept her eyes forward. “Certainly. It is always sad when you can do nothing to save a life.”

“I saw you, you know.” His tone was low and confidential.

She halted and turned to face him, a jolt of fear icing her belly. “What on earth are you talking about?” She tilted her chin and gave him a haughty glare, pressing her lips together to stop their trembling. It was essential that this upstart learn nothing that could incriminate her.

His eyes twinkled with mischief. “You retrieved something from the bedside. Perhaps left on an earlier visit?”

Outrage flooded her, sending a wave of heat up into her cheeks. “How dare you! I’ve never laid eyes on Lord Lochmere until tonight.” Her thoughts raced. Denial was the key. She must make him believe he had seen nothing. “In any case, I cannot imagine what you are talking about.” She raised her brows and gave him her most sincere gaze. “Yes, I looked around his chamber. I wanted to see if there was an explanation for his sudden illness.” And there was, one she was never going to share.

He bowed and backed away. “Forgive my rudeness, milady. I was but jesting.”

“It was an ill-placed jest, for certain. Perhaps that kind of ribald prattle goes down well in rustic Highland hovels, but not here in civilized circles.” Picking up her skirts, she spun on her heels and marched away, anger fueling her retreat.

Drat the ball. She was in no mood to laugh and flirt and dance, to pretend she had nothing on her mind save merriment and pleasure. *I will feign an illness and go home, posthaste.* Halfway down the stairs, an alarming thought made her steps falter, forcing her to grip the banister so as not to fall. Were Rory MacGregor’s ill-bred remarks a cover for trying to find out what, if anything, she knew about Lochmere’s death? Was the salve in her pocket the one Rory had claimed was meant for Ogilvy?

After taking the carriage home, she sent it back to wait for Margaret. She changed out of her gown with the help of her maid, then put on a dressing robe and went upstairs to her workroom. The remembrance of Lochmere's death ached like a stabbing wound. She would not be able to sleep until she checked her records and inventory.

First she examined the salve tin from Lochmere's room for clues. It was hers and looked like all the others as far as she could tell. Unfortunately, she didn't number them when they were dispensed. Perhaps she should start doing so, she thought, at least with medicines that could be dangerous if misused.

Or if I mix them wrong. This horrible idea hit her stomach like a blow, and she leaned heavily on the counter. No. She couldn't have made a mistake. She'd prepared the salve dozens of times. And she was always especially careful when working with deadly ingredients, for her own sake as well as that of her patients.

With a sense that she was locking the stable door after the steed had already fled, she opened her fat recipe book and quickly leafed to the wolfsbane salve. Yes, it was as she remembered. A base of beeswax infused with comfrey and calendula and only a few drops of wolfsbane. Closing her eyes, she could see it engraved in her memory. She had made no mistake. She would stake her life on it.

But how did Lochmere get the tin? She hadn't prescribed it for him, that much she knew for certain. She pulled down the leather-bound journal that served as her sales ledger. Here she recorded each transaction, including the date, patient, medicine, and amount paid. Working backward, she found Rory MacGregor for Lord Ogilvy, Lady Fiona Ross, and Dr. Donaldson.

Dr. Donaldson. Although the doctor never treated her with more than cool disdain, he wasn't above purchasing medicines from her on occasion. He had sent his servant over several weeks ago, well before Lord Lochmere arrived in Edinburgh. However, that didn't mean the doctor hadn't given Lochmere the tin.

She could try questioning him, but that idea was fraught with peril. Even broaching the subject was likely to be perceived as intrusive. At any rate, he wouldn't admit to guilt, certainly not to her.

Although it would explain why he was so eager to call it a heart paroxysm. As the only doctor present, he could have diagnosed anything at all, anything palatable for the prince to swallow.

She stared at the tin, which shone innocently in the light of the single candle she'd sparked. Now that she'd taken it from the sickroom, no one would believe she'd found it there. Was that a mistake? But if someone else had discovered it, someone unfriendly, she might have fallen under suspicion for Lochmere's death.

"I thought you had a headache." Margaret stood in the doorway, the scent of perfume like a cloud around her. "I should have known you would run back to your workshop rather than dally with fine men."

"I have more on my mind than dancing with Highlanders." She pointed to the tin. "Lord Lochmere died tonight, and I think my salve killed him."

With a gasp, Margaret sank down onto a stool. "I thought it was his heart."

Isabelle detailed the events she'd witnessed and her shock at finding the tin at the bedside.

"If I understand you right," Margaret said after some thought, "the salve is deadly if too much is applied. So, it might have been an accident. Or worse, someone gave him the wrong instructions."

"That's the conclusion I have come to."

"Lochmere wasn't your patient, you say. Then someone else must have given it to him."

Isabelle paced in the small space. "That is exactly what I was thinking when you came in." She listed the salve's three most recent purchasers.

"That fine specimen Rory MacGregor cannot be guilty." Margaret sighed in mock ecstasy. "I refuse to believe it."

"I don't see how a handsome face precludes murderous intent," Isabelle said tartly. "But clearing him is an easy matter. I will ask Lord Ogilvy what he thinks of the salve."

"But what if Lord Ogilvy was the one who gave Lochmere the salve?" Margaret's eyes danced in glee. "Questioning him could be dangerous."

"You are enjoying this entirely too much, cousin." Isabelle gave her a stern look but held little hope it would successfully repress Margaret's enthusiasm. "Let us not forget, a man is dead, and I might hang for it."

Margaret clapped a hand to her cheek. "I am sorry, cousin." She shuddered. "What of Dr. Donaldson? He is a most unpleasant man, and his hands are cold."

Isabelle refrained from asking Margaret how she knew that particular fact and explained her thoughts and doubts about talking to him. "The least likely appears to be Lady Fiona Ross."

"She is loyal to the king, is she not? So, she is an enemy of Bonnie Prince Charlie and Lord Lochmere. There you have it."

"Margaret, please. Her political loyalties aside, there is no evidence she even knew Lochmere."

"That is true." A frown flitted across Margaret's face.

"What is it?"

"Something occurred to me. The salve is a chancy way to kill someone. What if he refused to use it or did not put on enough to cause injury?"

Ice trickled down Isabelle's spine. "Someone might have doctored it to ensure Lochmere's death."

"Exactly. It was but the delivery system."

Isabelle stared blankly at the tin. "How will we ever find out? Unless . . ." She went to her inventory shelves. The poisonous elixirs and oils were kept in a separate area on the top shelf to prevent mix-ups. At first glance, everything looked as usual. Then she noticed several bottles out of place. When she restored them to order, an empty space was revealed . . . precisely where a bottle of wolfsbane oil should have been.

"I still don't see how a sewing circle can help solve the mystery of Lochmere's death." Isabelle was so tired that her head was swimming, and the trek up Holyrood's grand staircase wasn't helping. She'd been awake all night, fretting about the disappearance of the poisonous oil. It was obvious, to her at least, what happened. Someone had used the oil to make the salve much stronger—and much more likely to cause death.

"You'll see." Margaret's smile was smug. "The ladies without doubt will have plenty to say about Lord Lochmere."

Isabelle put a detaining hand on Margaret's arm. "Please, not a whisper of our suspicions to anyone."

Margaret scowled. "Of course not. I'm no featherbrain."

"Sorry, cousin. You certainly are not." In fact, Isabelle was quite impressed with Margaret's shrewdness. She had quickly grasped Isabelle's precarious position and the need to tread lightly when probing for the truth.

A guard directed them to where women had gathered in an

anteroom, sitting at work in a circle of chairs arranged near a cozy fire. A table holding refreshments and a tea urn sat close to hand.

Brenda Morrison waved as they entered. "Good afternoon, my dears. We saved seats for you." She pointed to two empty chairs next to her.

Isabelle and Margaret settled in their places, greeting the other dozen or so women of the Edinburgh nobility. While they included a girl of sixteen and someone's venerable grandmother, most were between eighteen and thirty.

"So glad ye could join us," the grandmother said. "Many hands make light work."

Brenda grabbed four-foot lengths of white ribbon from a basket. "Grannie already cut these for us. You need to fold them into even loops and stitch." She demonstrated and then gave them each a threaded needle. The finished product looked like a child's pinwheel.

Isabelle studied her ribbon dubiously. Her talents did not lie in the domestic arts.

Margaret picked up her needle and began to whip the stitches, her fingers moving deftly as she folded the ribbon. "Come on, Isabelle, it is very easy, even for a novice seamstress like you."

"I will give it a try. But I warn you, my efforts will be fit only for an Englishman."

They all laughed appreciatively at this witticism.

After they worked in silence for a few moments, Grannie said, "Och, we had a wee bit of commotion last night." She tsk-tsked. "Lord Lochmere dead as a doornail."

"A good thing, for certain!" one girl exclaimed. "He was a rare one for catching a lass unawares."

"You too?" Brenda raised her brows. "Before I knew what was what, he—" She puckered up her lips comically. "And me an engaged woman!"

The women burst into giggles, nudging each other with elbows.

At these frank remarks, Isabelle glanced toward the doorway to make sure no one was listening. She wasn't sure how the prince would react to this slander of his supporter's reputation. Although it wasn't slander if true.

"Isabelle witnessed his death," Margaret said to Isabelle's dismay. "She was in the sickroom with him until the end."

That drew all eyes to her. "Do tell," someone said.

She shifted uncomfortably in her seat, shooting Margaret a glare. What could she say? She certainly wasn't going to tell them about the salve.

"There is not much to tell, I am afraid. When I saw him fall, I thought I might be able to help. Everyone else thought he was drunk, you see."

"'Tis what I thought," Brenda said. "And he was not the only one." She chuckled.

A discussion of the abhorrent behavior of inebriated nobles ensued, and Isabelle hoped they would drop the topic of Lochmere.

No such luck. "So, did he die in your arms, Isabelle?" a woman asked, her eyes gleaming with mischief.

"I will wager he wanted to," another chimed in.

Someone hooted in glee.

"No, he most certainly did not," Isabelle said. "The men carried him to his chamber, but there was nothing to be done. He soon expired, but not before the priest administered the rites."

A few women crossed themselves, murmuring praise to God.

"What caused his death?" Brenda asked. She shook her head. "It happened so sudden-like."

"The doctor said it was his heart," Margaret said quickly, darting a glance at Isabelle under her eyelashes.

"That is correct, he did." Isabelle closed her mouth firmly, relieved at this neat skirting of the issue. Perhaps she could speak the barest truth and still manage to glean information. The fewer people who knew of her possible involvement, the better.

"God forgive me, but I am not saddened by his death," Grannie said, her needle moving so fast it was a blur. "He left Scotland under a cloud decades ago. Many prayed he would never return."

"What did he do, Grannie?" someone asked.

"These are all rumors, mind, so no tittle-tattle in the corridors." The older woman fixed each in turn with a stare.

Isabelle repressed a smile. It was humorous how people attempted to control gossip with such warnings. It was like controlling the tide's surge with a sandbank.

Grannie stopped sewing and sat back to tell her tale. "The Lochmeres are a sept of the Fraser clan. They hark from the shores of the Moray Firth, where the family seat, Lochmere Castle, sits high on a cliff."

Everyone settled down to listen to the older woman's story.

"They are a family of blackhearts, a conniving bunch who thieved their way into a fortune. They own all the land you can see from the top of the castle's highest tower, rich valleys and grazing grounds for their cattle and sheep." She fingered her skirt. "The wool from those sheep is among the finest produced in the Highlands. It is said that Mary, Queen of Scots, wore a gown made from it." She crossed herself at the mention of the ill-fated queen who'd ruled Scotland briefly before being executed in 1587.

"The family has always been canny when it comes to political matters, and the late Lord Lochmere was known for his fine footwork among the powerful. He did many favors for his friends, and they regarded him highly."

Isabelle listened closely for clues about who Lochmere's enemies might be. So far he sounded no worse than any other Scottish noble.

Then Grannie revealed the dirty laundry hidden by the lord's impeccable exterior. "It is said that Lochmere was a harsh master. They still talk about his cruel treatment of his tenants, how he turned families out to starve in the winter rains."

"For shame!" someone cried.

"His evil deeds were not limited to those beneath him. If another landowner made the mistake of crossing the lord, he would persecute him most mercilessly."

Isabelle revised her former assumption. "How was such a man admitted into the prince's inner circle?" she asked. With these revelations, she was beginning to think Lochmere's murder must have been in revenge for former wrongs.

"Och, he was very careful to never fall afoul of any Jacobites. Like many, he considered the Stuart line to be the rightful one. And with his wealth and powerful friendships, he was welcome in the exiled court."

"Why did he leave Scotland, then, if he was so well set up here?" someone asked.

Grannie pursed her lips. "The story is not suitable for young ears."

"Come on, Grannie," Brenda said. "We are all of age." Her gaze fell on the teenager. "Well, almost." She leaned toward the girl. "Cover your ears."

After the girl complied, Grannie said, "He forcibly married a widow and shut her in a tower. That's all I will say about the matter."

The women gasped in horror. Isabelle shuddered at all that remained unsaid in Grannie's brief explanation. She needed to talk to her alone and learn more.

"Long enough," Brenda said, pulling the girl's hands from her ears. The girl blushed and picked up her sewing.

"He was a wicked one, all right," one woman said. "And I've heard something else about him, something recent." She glanced around to be sure all were listening. "Despite his staunch support of the Stuarts, he was suspected of being a spy for the King of England."

7

Creighton, Vermont
Present Day

Still fuming over Sandy Wallace's rudeness, Sofia drove slowly along the vendor area, searching for the food truck. Russ had promised she couldn't miss it, and he was right. She spotted it easily, parked between a clothing tent and a pottery vendor. It was shiny and in good repair but painted a blinding neon green and trimmed with white awnings.

Good thing we'll be inside or that thing would give me a headache. As an artist, Sofia was sensitive to color—much more so than most people, apparently. She parked as close to the back door as she could to make unloading easier and climbed out.

Outside the tent next door, a short, round woman carrying a box of tartan fabric looked up as Sofia inserted the key into the truck door. After setting the box down on a folding chair, she trotted over with a wave. "Hi there. I'm Laura Kelly, from Bluebell Farm. I weave tartan and grow herbs." Despite a broad smile, her gray eyes remained watchful behind oval wire-rimmed glasses.

A friend of Sandy's, perhaps? Sofia kept her tone neutral as she said, "I saw your farm earlier. Beautiful place. I'm Sofia Parker, of . . ." She didn't even have a name for her business. "Sofia's Confectionery."

"Are you entering the shortbread contest?" Laura frowned, tossing her long blond braid into place.

Sofia turned back toward the door and twisted the key. "Yes. I guess I'm . . . how did Sylvia put it? Oh, yes. I'm taking Madelaine's place. Not that it was my intention." She pulled down on the handle and tugged. "Excuse me. I've got a lot to do before the fair opens."

"Hold on," Laura said, her voice trembling. "I didn't mean to get off on the wrong foot. It's just that Madelaine was one of my closest friends."

Sympathy welled up in Sofia's chest. "Oh. I'm so sorry for your loss." She stepped back down onto the ground. "I heard she died suddenly."

Laura blinked back tears, her eyes fixed on the ground near Sofia's feet. "Yes, she did. Right where you're standing, actually."

Involuntarily Sofia jumped back, a vision of a woman sprawled dead on the ground flashing into her mind. "That's awful. Were you here?"

"No, unfortunately." Laura found a tissue and wiped her eyes. "If I had been, maybe I could have helped her. I was in Connecticut for a Scottish event there. I guess Madelaine had come out here to check out the location. She hadn't been feeling well, so she missed Connecticut." After a pause, she sighed. "The games won't be the same without her. For the past ten years, we booked spots next to each other."

"Ten years? I take it she was an experienced baker." *And a tough act to follow.*

"Very much so. One of the best. Actually, she was . . ." Laura shook herself, as though coming out of deep thought. Her tone became brisk. "I'm sorry, you have a lot to do." She turned and walked toward her tent. "And so do I."

"Nice to meet you," Sofia called after her. *What had Laura started to say?* Oh well. It was none of her business. She had enough to do, minding her own.

Stepping inside the truck was like entering a stainless steel cave. She flipped the light switch despite the sunlight flooding through a long window to her right. *Good, the power is on.* Everything appeared surprisingly pristine, she was relieved to see, with a faint odor of lemon-scented soap still hanging in the air. *What was I expecting? Blood?*

A double oven, stove top, fridge, work counter, and storage cupboards lined the left wall. To the right was a work counter with more storage underneath. The long window slid open for customer service, and Sofia could envision racks with baked goods for sale stacked beside it. Straight ahead was a bay of triple sinks with handwashing and mop sinks nearby. Sofia checked to be sure the water was working. She'd been lucky to get a site with water hookup. Otherwise, she would have needed water deliveries to fill the truck's tank.

Despite the kitchen's apparent cleanliness, she decided to wash everything down again. That way she could be certain the surfaces were sanitary and her food was safe to eat. Sylvia had mentioned something about a health inspection, and Sofia intended to ace it.

After retrieving her cleaning supplies from the SUV, she discovered she needed to turn on the propane tank to get hot water. While waiting for it to heat, she decided to check all the cupboards and make sure they were empty.

All of the main storage areas were empty, including the bulkheads over the sink, with not a crumb or wrapper to be found. But when she checked the broom closet, a narrow slit of an opening, she found more than a mop and broom. A brightly colored cosmetic bag sat on the top shelf next to a half-full box of plastic gloves. Curious, she pulled it down.

The bag contained hair elastics, a tiny wooden brush, a tin of so-called natural lip balm, and pens. These were probably Madelaine's personal items, overlooked when the truck was cleaned. That notion made a tingle run down her spine.

The last item in the bag was a white plastic pill bottle with the label "Bluebell Farm—Women's Health Supplements." Laura's farm. Maybe she made them for Madelaine.

Sofia popped the lid and the tang of dried herbs hit her nose. She shook the bottle and peered in. There were three or four capsules left. She dropped the bottle back into the bag and zipped it shut. She thought she probably should throw it away, but for now she'd put it back on the shelf. Maybe Laura would want it.

"What do you think, Mom? Is it okay?" Wynter's voice was both proud and anxious.

Sofia turned her attention from the display case she was stocking to the sign Wynter had carefully lettered with colored chalks on a portable blackboard. It read, "Sofia's Scrumptious Scottish Treats. Lemon Tarts, Cranberry Scones, Oatmeal Cakes, Raisin Squares." The edges and corners were embellished with a design of thistles and ribbons.

"It's beautiful, Wynter. Go ahead and take it outside. We're about ready to open."

"Good job, Wynter," Vanessa chimed in. She was loading bills and change into the cash register. "I'll do the first shift so you can go watch the sheepdog trials."

Wynter grinned. "Really? Thanks, Vee. Dad said he has a surprise for us. I can't wait to see what it is." She picked up the sign and ran outside, her shoes clattering on the food truck steps.

"Thanks for helping, Vanessa. I know it'd be more fun checking out the other booths and displays. Not to mention the animals."

Vanessa turned the sign on the window to Open. "I can do that later. I'm happy to earn some money for my college fund." She threw her mother a sly smile. "And for shopping and that car I still want to buy." Sofia was paying her kids for helping in the truck even though they'd all offered to work before she mentioned an hourly wage.

"Speaking of shopping, there is a lot of tartan out there," Sofia observed.

Vanessa rolled her eyes. "Ugh, no. I haven't worn plaid since grade school."

Sofia poured two glasses of iced coffee, added milk and sugar, and handed Vanessa one.

"Thanks." Vanessa took a long swallow, then set it down. "Goodie. Our first customer."

A dark-haired teenage boy dressed in a kilt and a polo shirt stood at the window. "Hi, I'd like a raisin square, please." Then his eyes widened. "Vanessa?"

"Justin? What are you doing here?" Her gaze traveled to his bare legs. "I didn't know you wore kilts."

"I don't usually." He shifted from foot to foot, clearly uncomfortable. "I'm here for the fiddle championship."

"Wow. That's awesome. I knew you were in band but not that you played competitively." She reached for a raisin square, using a square of bakery tissue paper to pick it up the way Sofia had taught her, and slid it into a waxed paper bag.

A big grin broke out across his face. "I came close to winning last year. First runner-up. Wish me luck."

"Sure. Wish us luck too. My mom's in the shortbread contest." She pointed to the big banner hanging over the midway aisle that read, "Best Biscuits Best Shortbread Contest: You Choose the Best."

His eyes darted from the banner to Sofia, standing beside Vanessa in the window. "Really? Cool."

"Fairgoers get a say in the contest," Vanessa said. "So come by and vote this afternoon."

He placed his payment on the shelf. "I'll do better than that. I'll get all the fiddle players to vote for you." Vanessa handed him his treat, and with a nod he sauntered off into the crowd.

"Did you hear that, Mom?" Vanessa hugged Sofia. "We're going to get lots of votes, I know it!"

Sofia wasn't sure if the kids' plan verged on collusion, but what the heck, it was sweet of him to offer. Wasn't that what friends did—support each other? Besides, the initial vote was the preliminary to the finals, which would be judged by professionals.

Business was brisk the rest of the morning, and both Sofia and Vanessa were kept busy serving customers and ringing up sales.

"Gosh, I'm going to have to plan on double batches tomorrow," Sofia said, making a note to get more ingredients. "I hope what we have will last through the end of the day."

Vanessa glanced at the half-empty pastry case. "No kidding. But you're making shortbread soon, right? That'll help fill the shelves."

Sofia grimaced. "I think we have to give that away." She peered out into the midway. "Mr. Best is supposed to be coming around and telling us about the contest pretty soon."

Vanessa pointed to a group in front of Laura's tent. "Could that be him, by any chance?"

Sofia leaned a little farther out of the window. A balding man wearing glasses and dressed in a suit stood in the midway speaking to a small group, including Sandy Wallace. Judging from everyone's attentive posture as he spoke, she guessed that he was indeed Barclay Best from Best Biscuits.

One of the women broke away and beelined for Sofia's window. As she drew closer, Sofia noticed she was middle-aged and trim with close-cropped hair, and she was wearing a dress and heels, an outfit far too formal for the casual fairgrounds. She clasped a clipboard to her chest.

"Are you Sofia Parker?" the woman asked after glancing at her clipboard.

Sofia smiled, although her pulse was racing. The contest had begun. "Yes, I am. Are you with Best Biscuits?"

The woman held out her tiny hand and Sofia reached down and clasped it. "Yes. I'm Donna Roberts, Mr. Best's assistant and taster."

"Taster?" For a wild moment, Sofia pictured Donna trying every dish before passing it to Mr. Best to ensure that it hadn't been poisoned.

Donna's smile was smug. "Oh yes. I'm his best palate. I can parse a recipe in ten seconds. Twenty, max." She wagged a finger. "And I always detect artificial flavorings."

Sofia attempted a laugh. "Don't worry. I don't use any artificial flavor. Especially not in my shortbread."

The woman beckoned to her. "Well, come on down. Mr. Best is going to go over the contest rules."

Sofia took off her apron. "Can you watch the counter, Vanessa? I'll be right back."

"Sure thing, Mom." She lowered her voice to a whisper. "Go get 'em."

Outside the truck, the sun was beating down relentlessly and Sofia immediately felt sweat trickling between her shoulder blades. *Oh, don't let my deodorant fail now!*

After joining the small group, Donna made the introductions. Barclay Best pursed his lips and nodded, hands clasped behind his back, checking Sofia over as if able to determine her cooking skills by sight alone. The other contestants were Annie Bowers of Granny's Green Mountain Bakery, a couple—both named Ronnie Ross—of Ross Pastry, the cadaverous Archie MacKenzie of MacKenzie & Sons, and Sandy Wallace. Sandy glared at Sofia with a snarled, "I've had the pleasure." Her tone implied quite the opposite.

"Welcome, all," Barclay said. His voice was dry and on the monotonous side. "I'm excited to be here and to see what delightful confections you'll create for us."

"We're so excited to have you here, Mr. Best," Sandy said, her voice a sultry coo at odds with her forbidding demeanor. The flirtatious expression on her face was ghastly.

Not to be outdone, Ronnie Ross, the wife, rudely elbowed Annie out of the way. "That's right, sir. Yes sir." Sofia half expected her to salute. Studying the couple, she was amused to notice that not only did they have the same name, they were similar in height and build. *And their builds are like bowling balls,* she thought.

Not to be outdone, Annie, a tiny older woman in a housedress and apron, elbowed Ronnie in turn. "Mr. Best, we're honored to have ye at our humble games," she said in her charming Scottish accent.

Barclay barely cracked a smile. "Your enthusiasm is appreciated." He scanned the group, the sun glancing off his glasses. "We expect the rules to be followed to the letter." He held up one finger. "One. No artificial ingredients can be used. Two. All food service protocols must be followed. Three. You must make the cookies yourself, here on-site." His face was stern. "Is that understood?"

"Yes, Mr. Best," the group said in unison, exactly like a scolded elementary class.

"Good. The contest has three stages. Today we will have fairgoers vote on their favorite cookies. That will eliminate one of you. In two days, we will have a local panel decide. Another pair will be voted off the island." Best chuckled.

Everyone dutifully laughed.

"By then, we will be down to two of you. Our professional tasters, including Ms. Roberts, will make the final decision." All eyes swiveled to Donna. Sandy edged closer to her, as if hoping to use friendship to influence her decision.

For a long moment, no one said anything. Finally, Barclay clapped his hands. "That's it. Ladies—and gentleman—start your ovens. May the best *Best* baker win!"

The contestants scattered like startled pigeons. Sofia hurried back to the food truck. It was time to start mixing shortbread. Her recipe required chilling the dough for an hour.

"How'd it go while I was gone?" she asked Vanessa as she tied on a fresh apron.

"After you left, I heard someone making noise behind the food truck—you know, doing something back there. So I thought I should check it out."

"Was it one of the fair workers? That's where our electric hookup is."

"Yeah, I think so. At least that's what he said. He was there to make sure everything was hooked up."

"That sounds pretty normal to me."

"First of all, he wasn't anywhere near the hookup. And he had a mouse in his pocket. I saw it peeking out." She wiggled her nose. "It was twitching its whiskers."

8

Edinburgh, Scotland
September 1745

Isabelle's thoughts whirled around the woman's accusation. *Could Lord Lochmere have been a spy?* This would provide a definite motive for murder. The Jacobites were a fiercely loyal bunch, and an enemy in the camp would be dealt with harshly. Too much was riding on the prince's claim to the throne. Failure now likely would mean the death of the Jacobite cause forever.

"Where did you get that information?" Margaret asked. "Lochmere was well known for his allegiance to Prince Charlie."

The woman shrugged. "Where does the wind come from? The rumor was bandied about the moment Lochmere set foot on Scottish soil."

"Yes," another put in, "they say his greed far exceeded his loyalty."

"I am confused," Isabelle said. "I witnessed the prince's sorrow at Lochmere's passing. Why would he grieve the death of a traitor?"

"Perhaps the whispers did not reach the prince," Brenda said.

"It is all moot now," Grannie said. "The man is dead, and good riddance." She glanced around. "Do ye think the serving maid might bring us a wee bit of tea? I am dry as a bone."

The young girl went to fetch the maid, and the others chattered and laughed with their neighbors. Isabelle pretended to concentrate on her mangled cockade. This afternoon she'd heard more than one reason for Lochmere's murder—if indeed murder it was. Evicted tenants, local enemies, mistreated women . . . the list seemed to go on and on. He had been surrounded by enemies here; it would have served him better to remain in France.

She wondered if she should drop the entire issue. After all, no one else seemed to suspect anything. That should be a relief to her. Life could go on as usual, with concerns consisting only of assisting her patients and learning more about herbal remedies. For instance, the new botanical garden had some interesting plants she wanted to investigate.

Then she remembered the missing wolfsbane oil. She couldn't ignore such a threat. Someone deliberately tried to implicate her. If she didn't learn who it was, she would be vulnerable to accusations that might strike at any time. Accusations of murder—and the hangman's noose if she was found guilty.

She nestled her hands in her lap to stop their shaking. Margaret glanced over. "Are you all right?" she whispered.

Isabelle shook her head, unable to speak. She glanced around the circle, praying no one would notice her sudden distress.

Margaret patted her knee. "Let me get you a cup of tea," she whispered. "Then you and I will get to the bottom of this."

Isabelle watched her cousin sashay over to the tea table, exchanging jests and remarks along the way. She was so fortunate to have Margaret in her corner. Her cousin's robust good sense provided a bolstering effect on her own flagging courage.

"Here you are, my love." Margaret handed her a teacup and saucer. While still bent over, she said in a low voice, "The maid wants to talk to us. So drink up."

Isabelle obeyed, her pulse thrumming with excitement and dread. Their investigation was under way.

After the sewing group disbanded, Isabelle and Margaret waited for the maid to return to clear the dishes. She seemed startled to see someone still there, but relaxed when she recognized Margaret. She sketched a curtsy. "How may I help you, miladies?"

"Come sit with us," Margaret said with a wave. The maid did so reluctantly, glancing over her shoulder as if frightened that someone might catch her lounging instead of working. "Bess . . . that is your name, correct?" The maid nodded. "My cousin, Lady Isabelle, has some questions for you."

The maid's full cheeks colored. "What kind of questions, milady?"

Isabelle thought quickly. She hadn't expected to interview someone so soon and she wasn't quite prepared. She also needed to be careful since there was no way to prevent the maid from gossiping with the other servants. Then she thought of something so outrageous it might work.

She smiled in what she hoped was an ingratiating manner. "Bess, do you support the prince's cause?" Margaret shot her a confused frown that she ignored.

Bess looked taken aback. "Of course I do, milady. That was a condition of my employment."

"As well it should be. It wouldn't do to have spies here, right in the heart of the prince's headquarters, would it?" Isabelle did her best to sound authoritative. She kept her eyes on Bess but she sensed Margaret shifting in her seat and knew that she had caught on to her ploy.

"No, milady, of course not." The girl's tone was adamant. A crease appeared between her brows. "My loyalty is not in question, is it? For I swear—"

Isabelle put her hand up to stem the maid's assurances. "I believe you. But there was someone else here at Holyrood who might not have quite the same level of devotion."

Bess sucked in a breath, her eyes like saucers. "No, milady, say it is not so." She glanced around to make sure no one was listening before leaning forward to whisper, "Is it another servant?"

"No. Worse, much worse." Isabelle also dropped her voice to a whisper. "Lord Lochmere."

"Lord Lochmere?" The maid crossed herself. "May he rest in peace."

Margaret spoke up. "Earlier you said you were responsible for making up his room."

Bess nodded. "I do all the noblemen's rooms. Well, along with Ella." She gestured at the cups and saucers sitting on the table. "And we do meal service too, as you can see. They keep us running from dawn until dusk."

"So you saw Lord Lochmere quite often, then," Isabelle said.

"Oh yes. Starting with tea service every morning first thing."

"Then maybe you can help us. My cousin and I have been charged with helping the prince figure out who Lochmere's enemy contacts were." Isabelle delivered this bald lie with as straight a face as she could muster. Inwardly she repented, hoping her intention of finding the murderer outweighed the deceit.

"We need to know who visited him in his chambers," Margaret said.

Bess blinked. "Oh my. That is quite a task. You see, Lord Lochmere had many visitors." She waved her hand. "The palace is full of people day and night. I won't be sad when they all leave, I tell you. Though I will remember serving His Majesty long as I live." She gave a deep sigh. "God save our future king."

"Well, serve him now by helping us. Think, Bess. Did anyone unusual visit? Someone not involved in the prince's campaign?" Although Isabelle knew that the poisoner could indeed be someone else close to the prince—Rory MacGregor for instance—discovering if any outsiders visited Lochmere might confirm or deny the possibility that a tenant or relative was responsible.

Bess tilted her head, thinking. "The only visitor who stands out in my memory is a beautiful woman with bright red hair."

She grinned. "Besides the soldiers in kilts."

Margaret fingered her auburn curls. "Redheaded beauties are a dime a dozen in Edinburgh." She winked. "And right now, so are handsome lads wearing the plaid."

Her cousin was right. The maid's information wasn't nearly as helpful as Isabelle had hoped. They would have to keep making inquiries—discreetly, of course.

"This is cozy." Sebastian Ripa pulled back his chair and sat opposite Isabelle. She had decided to serve dinner in the drawing room on a gateleg table pulled up in front of a roaring fire instead of in the vast and drafty dining room. It was only the two of them, after all. Besides, this room, with its restful green-paneled walls and elegant but comfortable furniture, was her favorite place in the house.

Isabelle served her father a slice of veal-and-ham pie. "I think we should make a habit of eating in here, at least during the winter." She added boiled potatoes and carrots to the plate and placed it in front of him.

He reached both hands out to the blaze. "I agree." Rather than dig into his meal, he stared into the leaping flames.

"Are you all right, Papa?" Isabelle studied his handsome, familiar features, noticing new lines bracketing his mouth and eyes.

He gave her a weary smile. "Just tired. I have been playing almost every night at Holyrood, which is a good thing for the purse but not so good for my health, not at my age." He picked up his fork and stabbed a potato.

"You are not old, Papa," she said automatically, taking a bite of the warm, savory pie. Their cook made the most delicious flaky pastry.

"At any rate, we symphony musicians are enjoying the windfall of soirees and balls held at Prince Charles's court."

"It has been a whirl." Isabelle couldn't remember a time when the staid city had been so lively.

The maid entered the room carrying a silver tray. "A letter for you, milord."

Sebastian grimaced but said thank you as he took the envelope. Being called "lord" annoyed him, Isabelle knew. His late wife had been the one with the title, but the servants insisted on addressing him respectfully as a nobleman.

He popped the wax seal and quickly scanned the contents, then tossed the letter onto the tablecloth.

"Another symphony engagement?"

"For a change, no." He took a sip of cider. "An invitation to dinner from Lady Fiona Ross."

"Oh my. Again?" Lady Fiona persistently invited her father to the soirees and dinners she hosted weekly. "Doesn't she know you were married to a staunch Jacobite?" Fiona's maiden name was Kerr, and the clans Kerr and Ross were both loyal to the king.

"Of course she knows. Bad blood between the MacDonalds and the Rosses goes back decades." He shrugged, lips quirked in an amused smile. "I think she is seeking posthumous revenge upon Fenella. They were rivals, you know, not only in politics but in love."

"But Papa, that is bizarre. Deranged, even." Despite her words, she could understand why the widowed Lady Fiona was interested in her father. He was blessed with the aquiline good looks and olive skin of his Italian forebears, which made him stand out in pale-skinned Scotland. In addition, he was a highly talented musician and composer as well as a true gentleman.

"Lady Fiona is a wee bit touched, I think." He shook his head. "If only your dear mother had lived to witness Prince Charles's return. She would be right out front, leading the charge for his restoration. She feared nothing."

"I wish I was that brave." Isabelle loved hearing stories about Fenella, but most of them left her feeling like a pale imitation of her mother's magnificence.

"But you are, daughter. Not everyone would have the courage to challenge a physician in a diagnosis the way you do quite frequently. Am I right? I am also certain if you had been admitted at the university, you would have been a top student." His dark eyes beamed warm approval.

"Thank you, Papa. I do love my work."

"Don't work too hard. I was surprised you didn't return to the ball last night. Margaret and your other friends certainly appeared to be enjoying themselves."

Isabelle put down her utensil, what remained of her appetite fleeing. She hadn't seen her father long enough to tell him about her presence at Lochmere's deathbed and the discovery of the salve. "I have something alarming to tell you."

While he made a pretense of eating, she told him everything, from the details of Lochmere's death to the interview with the maid that afternoon. As she expected, he honed in on the most salient facts. "Someone stole a vial of oil, you say? Right out of the house?"

"Yes, they did. I keep a careful inventory of all my stock so I don't run out of anything."

"That is troubling." He rubbed his chin, thinking. "We could question the servants, but I doubt they let anyone into your workroom without your knowledge."

"I know. I cannot figure out how the thief did it."

"They may have come in while everyone gathered to watch the prince enter the city. The servants went too, right?"

"Yes, they did." Isabelle thought back to the day, how the prince and his guard paraded down this very street, both sides lined with cheering citizens. The house probably had remained unlocked since everyone was standing outside nearby.

"If we knew who wanted Lochmere dead, that would lead us to the guilty party."

Isabelle laughed. "I suppose in most cases that would be a short list. But Lochmere had enemies everywhere. According to the stories I heard, he was a most despicable person. They even think he might have been a spy!"

"That is a serious charge indeed. And it expands the lot of possible killers to nearly every Jacobite."

"In the interests of expediency, I narrowed the suspects to those who purchased my salve. If they were not involved, then we must look further afield." She ticked them off. "Lord Ogilvy, Dr. Donaldson, Lady Fiona."

"All highborn or well connected. Perhaps it would be best to drop it." He pointed his fork at Isabelle. "You could be in danger if you pursue the issue. Let it rest in peace, like Lord Lochmere."

He was probably right. But for the first time in her life, she was going to disobey her darling papa. She had to find out who killed Lochmere or else live under the shadow of his death for the rest of her life.

"Lady Isabelle," the guard announced, standing back to let her enter Dr. Donaldson's Holyrood suite. Although he saw patients at an office in his town house, he had moved to the palace while the court was in residence so he could serve the prince.

Dr. Donaldson sat behind a desk, scratching notations in a ledger. He was dressed all in black as was his custom. He glanced up as Isabelle approached and set his quill in the holder. "Good afternoon, Lady Isabelle." He nodded toward the basket she carried. "I trust that is my order?"

"It is." Isabelle set the basket she carried on the desk. She'd used the doctor's order as a pretext to visit him instead of sending a servant as was customary. She reached inside and pulled out several bottles and set them on the desk. "Lungwort syrup. White willow tincture." He'd wanted two of willow, no doubt to assist those whose heads ached after celebrating too heavily. She added tins of salve. "Comfrey for gout. Primrose for wounds."

"Very good." He picked up the bottle of headache remedy and examined the label. "I see you put the suggested dose on here."

What a perfect opening. "I've decided to start doing that, especially for medicines patients take or apply on their own. My wolfsbane salve, for instance, which as you know can be dangerous if used too frequently."

He set the bottle down. "It is a good idea. I often write out dosages for patients. Except when they cannot read, of course." He made a face. "Which is still the case with far too many, I'm afraid." Although Edinburgh's education rate was higher than most places in England, many in the lower classes remained illiterate.

Now that the subject was broached, Isabelle felt she could press further. "How is your patient doing, the one who is using the wolfsbane salve?"

The doctor appeared puzzled. "Fine, I am sure. He has not been back since I gave him the medicine."

"Who was he, out of curiosity?"

"Mr. Sloan, the landlord of the White Hart tavern on Grassmarket. Rheumatism in his joints was interfering with his work. He is on his feet all day and most of the night."

"I can understand that. Glad I could help." The doctor didn't seem to be deceiving her, so she moved on to address her main concern directly. "Lord Lochmere's death was so dreadful. And on such a happy occasion too." She put on an appropriate expression of dismay. "I'm not sure I have recovered from the shock."

The doctor began to fiddle with the medicine bottles, lining them up in a row. "Yes, it certainly was a distressing turn of events." He shrugged. "Unfortunately, these things happen, especially to men of Lochmere's age and habits."

"Was there any warning?" Isabelle moved slightly closer. "I wish to know so I can understand the illness and perhaps prevent another sudden death."

Donaldson stroked his beard. "I am not sure what you mean."

She didn't believe that for an instant. "Was he in good health? Were there symptoms that in retrospect would indicate a heart problem?"

He remained silent, so she listed what she learned reading a medical text purchased from a secondhand book dealer. "Pains in the chest. A heavy sensation here." She patted her breastbone. "Rapid pulse. Shortness of breath."

"I know what the symptoms are." Rising from his chair, he drew himself up to his full height and leaned toward her, reminding Isabelle of a looming crow. "I am surprised that you do . . . as an *herbalist*." He spoke this last as though it were an epithet.

Isabelle bit back angry words. His dismissive attitude was all too familiar. She experienced it often when dealing with doctors. Not only were women considered inferior in reasoning ability, but she represented the long tradition of healers jostling with university-educated physicians for supremacy in the medical arts. Unfortunately for Donaldson, many still put more faith in the old ways than in doctors. To add insult, physicians relied upon skilled herbalists to treat their patients, and unless they wanted to learn compounding, they would continue to do so.

"I can read," she said as mildly as possible. "And I wish to learn as much as possible so I can relieve suffering. Surely that is what you want also?"

Surprisingly, he backed down. "Of course. But please, leave the diagnosing to me."

She dipped in a curtsy, masking her irritation with a false smile. "Certainly, doctor."

"Lord Lochmere's quick death was odd. He appeared to be in robust health. His only complaint was a minor rash." The doctor shrugged. "I suggested he bathe the area with mare's milk." He picked up a salve tin and examined it closely, probably more for something to do than out of interest, she guessed.

She needed to be certain. "The condition didn't require a prescription?"

"Not in my opinion. So, you see, his sudden demise was as much a surprise to me as it was to everyone else."

"Especially Lord Lochmere," she said wryly. She took a deep breath, praying that she wasn't making a mistake. "My first impression was that he might have been poisoned."

The salve tin dropped to the desk with a clatter. "Poison? Why on earth would you think such a thing?"

"He said he felt cold . . . and his breathing was labored. Some poisons do that." She bit back further explanation. "I guess I was wrong."

His smile was smug. "Like I said, leave the diagnosing to me." He picked up his pen. "Please excuse me. I have a lot to do."

As she picked up her basket to go, she realized that although she still didn't like Donaldson, she had heard nothing to indicate he gave the salve to the dead man. To be certain, she should pay a call on the landlord of the tavern. Or send someone she trusted. The White Hart wasn't a savory spot for a woman alone.

9

Creighton, Vermont
Present Day

Someone tapped on the metal counter outside the food truck. "Can I get some service here?"

Vanessa was handling the customers while Sofia was mixing shortbread dough on autopilot, lost in thought about the mouse Vanessa saw in the workman's pocket. *Why would anyone carry a rodent around?* She shuddered instinctively.

"Excuse me, ma'am," the voice said more loudly. "You might be a big-shot baker, but that doesn't mean you can ignore the common folk."

That snapped Sofia out of it. Her husband stood at the window, a welcome sight. "Jim! You're back."

"Yes, we are. Lunch break." He waved several greasy paper sacks emitting savory smells.

"Great timing. I'm finished here for a while." Sofia put plastic wrap over the bowls and stowed them in the refrigerator. Although they needed a good hour to chill, she had plenty of time to bake the shortbread before the three o'clock contest deadline.

"Mom, we have a surprise for you." Matthew's eyes and the top of his head were all Sofia could see over the counter.

"A good one, I hope."

He jumped up a few times, trying to get a better view of his mother. "Yes, it is. Come on out."

"Go ahead, Mom." Vanessa made a shooing motion. "I'll take a break after you eat."

Sofia took off her apron again. "Thanks, hon. I won't be long. Then it'll be Wynter's turn to help anyway."

Outside the food truck, Jim was setting up folding cloth chairs with the help of another man, a big, burly fellow with a crew cut and freckles.

"Hello," Sofia said. "I'm Jim's wife, Sofia Parker."

The man glanced up and gave her a wide smile, a familiar twinkle in his blue eyes. "Hey. I'm Brian Sinclair." He thrust out a meaty paw to shake. "Jim's long-lost cousin." He laughed. "What did we figure? Three or four times removed, Jim?"

At his words, Sofia realized why his eyes seemed familiar. He had to be related to Jim, however distantly. She liked him immediately. "I'm very glad to meet you."

Wynter and Luke came barreling around the corner of the truck, each holding a leash attached to a border collie. "Hi, Mom," Wynter called. "Aren't these dogs great?"

"Yeah, Mom, this one is a champion sheepherder." Luke's grin was ecstatic. He pointed to a blue ribbon attached to the dog's collar. The dog panted, his friendly expression appearing to grin too.

Jim was extending the legs on a folding table to hold the food. "They both belong to Brian. That's where we ran into each other, at the trials."

"Lucky break for me." Brian set the paper bags on the table and pulled out wrapped sandwiches. "These guys have been a big help with the dogs."

"Should we tie them up over here?" Luke asked, pointing to a power pole. At Brian's nod, they looped the leads around.

Brian set down two water dishes. "Can I trouble you for some water?"

"Of course," Sofia said. "Wynter, can you please go in the truck and get a bunch of those bottled waters? For us and the dogs." She sat down in one of the chairs with a sigh of relief. She'd been on her feet since early in the morning.

"I got you a salad with chicken," Jim said, setting a clamshell container on the table along with a packet of dressing and a fork. "There's one for Vanessa too." He handed it to Matthew. "Take that in to her, will you, please?"

Sofia opened the salad and squished dressing over the greens. "Now that I've stopped moving, I'm starving." She took her first bite, enjoying the tangy blend of flavors.

His errand complete, Matthew dashed back out of the truck and grabbed his sandwich. "We got sausage subs." After chewing his first bite, he looked puzzled. "It tastes like regular sausage."

"Why wouldn't it, bud?" Jim asked.

"'Cause it's Scottish."

Everyone laughed. "Not everything is different," Wynter said. "Scottish people eat regular food too. And so do Scottish dogs." Laughing, she pulled her chair a little farther away from the dogs, who were both pining for a taste of her sandwich.

"Don't let those rascals beg," Brian said. "They only eat twice a day."

"What are their names?" Sofia asked. Of medium size, they were cute, with black and white fluffy fur. One sported a black patch over one eye, and the other had black over both.

"That one is Fergus," Luke said, pointing to the dog with one patch. "He's old. The other is Finnean. He's the champion now."

"But Fergus used to be, right, Brian?" Wynter's voice rose in defense of the retired contender.

"Yes, he's Finnean's father. He won many blue ribbons in his day."

Laura Kelly came out of the back of her tent. She gave the

group a wave, then her eyes widened in recognition. "Hi, Brian. How did the trials go?"

Mid-bite, Brian chewed and swallowed. "They went great, thanks." He pointed at Finnean. "He won again."

"Congratulations." Laura's gaze fell on Sofia. "I didn't know you knew Brian." She moved closer and put a hand on his shoulder. "We go way back, don't we?"

He threw her a smile. "Sure do, since we both live here in Creighton."

"I didn't know Brian until today," Sofia said with a laugh. "He's Jim's distant cousin." She went around the circle and introduced everyone. "Laura weaves tartan, and she also grows herbs at Bluebell Farm." Madelaine had been one of Laura's customers, according to the bottle Sofia had found in the food truck. Maybe Madelaine had experienced a bad reaction to the supplement. Couldn't herbs interact with medicine, like any drug? That was one reason she was cautious about taking herbs beyond drinking the most innocuous herbal tea.

"I'm going to give some spinning lessons, if you're interested," Laura said to Wynter. "And a lesson in making peppermint tea."

Wynter glanced at her mother. "Can I, Mom? They both sound fascinating." Wynter tended to use pet words and her latest was *fascinating*.

"Of course you can. Maybe Vanessa would like to join you."

"I'll ask her." Wynter stood and put her sandwich wrapper in a nearby trash can. "I'm going to help with the window now." She bent over and gave each dog a thorough pat on the head. "I'll see you later, boys." She scurried into the food truck.

"Wash your hands," Sofia called.

"Yes, Mom." Wynter sighed heavily. "I know." The truck door slammed behind her.

Laura didn't seem in any hurry to go back to her tent. "So, Jim, if you're related to Brian, then you're a member of Clan Sinclair?"

Jim shook his head. "Not that I know of. My mother was a Gregg, and we're related through her side."

"Gregg is a family name of Clan MacGregor," Brian said. Stretching his mouth wide, he demolished the rest of his sandwich in one bite, much to Matthew and Luke's awe.

Sofia felt a jolt of excitement. "That's interesting. My Edinburgh ancestor was also connected to the MacGregors in 1745."

Brian's eyebrows rose in interest as he swallowed and then took a long swig of water to wash the food down. He balled up his wrapper and tossed it toward the trash can. It fell in neatly. The boys cheered, then attempted the same with their own wrappers. "A Rory MacGregor went to Edinburgh when Bonnie Prince Charlie took the city and fought with the Jacobites. Rory was the second son of a laird from Glen Orchy, way up in the northern Highlands."

Did the tartan in the quilt belong to Rory MacGregor? Sofia couldn't wait to read more of the entry to see if she could find out.

"I'm impressed," Jim said. "You know a lot about clan history, then."

Brian shrugged. "Enough to be dangerous. If you really want to talk to an expert, Dr. Benjamin Campbell is your guy. He's giving a lecture here at the games."

"I signed up for an appointment with him," Sofia said. "And with that endorsement, I'm really glad I did."

"Dr. Campbell is great," Laura said. "I love hearing him speak."

Sofia was surprised that Laura would leave her tent unattended for so long, particularly with a constant stream of customers wandering by.

Brian shared the thought. "Who's watching the store, Laura?"

"My niece, Mandy. If she needs me, she'll holler, I'm sure." Her gaze went to the midway. "Which might be any minute. Attendance is picking up." She waved vigorously. "Wendell! Wendell! Over here."

Brian let out a little groan. When Sofia glanced at him, he pretended great interest in the remaining contents of his water bottle. He didn't look around when a tall man wearing a kilt detached himself from the crowd and walked toward them. Vanessa stood in the doorway of the truck, staring blatantly, and Sofia realized why.

With his alert, confident carriage and striking good looks, Wendell resembled an actor striding out of a costume drama. To heighten the effect of his dramatic appearance, sunlight gilded his curly blond hair and glanced off the metal trimming of the bagpipes he carried tucked under one arm.

His voice was deep and sonorous. "Good afternoon, Laura." He nodded at her and then smiled at Sofia and her family. He ignored Brian, who continued to study his water bottle.

"Wendell MacKay, meet the Parkers." Laura fairly vibrated with pride at introducing her friend. "Wendell is one of the best bagpipers in New England. You'll see him playing throughout the games."

"Only in New England? Gee." Wendell grimaced in mock hurt, then winked at her.

Laura blushed and cast a sidewise glance at Brian. Feeling uncomfortable with the swirling undercurrents, Sofia rose to her feet. "This has been nice, but it's time for me to go make shortbread."

"I guess I'd better get back to my booth," Laura said. She put a hand on Wendell's arm. "Come with me? I'll put the kettle on."

The atmosphere deflated slightly after the duo walked away, and Vanessa disappeared back inside.

"I was kind of rude, wasn't I?" Brian said.

Sofia, on her way up the truck steps, paused and turned.

"Sorry about that." Brian grimaced.

"Well, I got the distinct feeling you don't care for Wendell," Jim said with a little laugh. Before Brian could say anything else, he turned to the boys. "Why don't you take the dogs for a quick walk? Down to the grandstand and back." Luke and Matthew jostled each other to be the first to reach the dogs. Then, leashes in hand, they trotted off.

Brian gritted his teeth. "Do you blame me? He stole Madelaine from me." His hand clenched the plastic water bottle so tightly it crunched. "We dated for over a year. Then he decided he liked her, and it was all over." His laugh was bitter. "He's quite the catch, can't you tell? All the ladies fall for his line."

Laura certainly seems interested in him. And supposedly she and Madelaine were good friends.

Jim patted Brian's shoulder. "That's rough, buddy. Do you see them together a lot?"

Brian's mouth opened, but nothing came out. Realizing that Jim didn't know who Madelaine was or that she was dead, Sofia said, "Jim, Madelaine died recently. She was the one scheduled to rent this truck, as a matter of fact."

Now Jim's mouth hung open. "Gosh, I'm sorry. I didn't know." He blinked his eyes rapidly, obviously regretting his faux pas.

"No reason why you should," Brian said, his voice hoarse. "I can barely believe it myself." His blue eyes were fierce as they met Sofia's gaze. "And she didn't have a heart problem. I don't care what the coroner said, Madelaine was in perfect health."

10

Edinburgh, Scotland
September 1745

"I have never visited a military camp before." Margaret shivered in excitement. "Thousands of men have gathered, I heard."

Isabelle had postponed her trip to the White Hart tavern to first travel with Margaret on horseback out of the city proper to see Lord Ogilvy in the nearby village of Duddingston, where Bonnie Prince Charlie's army was amassing.

"Frankly, I find it a little frightening," Isabelle said. Margaret gave her a questioning glance. "Not because of the soldiers, but because of what this all means." She nodded at the wagons and platoons and tradesmen thronging the once-quiet road to the tiny village. "War is really upon us."

Indeed, the mood in the city remained tense as Prince Charles prepared to launch the next stage of his campaign. An early battle against the English was easily won, and now his sights were set upon larger targets. Closer to home, a blockade around Edinburgh Castle held the English soldiers stationed there in check. But the truce was uneasy and could end at any time, thereby putting citizens directly in the line of fire.

"A justified war makes it all the more thrilling. Prince Charles is the rightful king." Margaret threw her a cheeky grin as she tapped her horse on the flank with her crop, urging it into a trot. "Let's race!"

Isabelle spurred her own mount. Soon they were pounding along neck and neck, whooping and laughing, earning both smiles and frowns from the people they passed.

"That was invigorating," Isabelle said, panting as their horses slowed to a walk. She inhaled deeply, enjoying the fresh air, so much sweeter than Edinburgh's burning coal fires and street odors. "We should go riding more often."

"Whew! I agree." Margaret fanned her face with her hand. "I forgot how lovely it is outside the city."

They ambled through a small gathering of cottages, past an inn and a church marking Duddingston proper, then out into countryside again. Isabelle pointed. "I think that is the camp over there."

Rows of white tents were strung across a wide hayfield now trampled into dust. Scores of men moved about the area, some marching in formation while others worked at various tasks. Corrals held horses and other beasts, and rows of wagons and carriages and carts sat to one side.

Sentries guarded the main entrance into the enclave, creating a slow-moving funnel of traffic in and out. As they drew closer, Isabelle noticed the guards exhibited a more relaxed demeanor than the stiff, unblinking formality displayed by English redcoats. Regardless, their belts bristled with dirks, swords, and pistols.

"What can I do for ye, lassie?" the guard asked when it was their turn. He scratched his nose with a none-too-clean forefinger and belched, obviously not feeling they were a great threat.

"We are here to see Lord Ogilvy," Isabelle said. "I understand he is out here today." They'd gone by Holyrood first and learned he'd left for the camp that morning.

The guard glanced them over and decided they were all right to enter. "Tie your horses here and go in on foot." He pointed. "You will find Lord Ogilvy in the officers' quarters."

All the tents looked alike from her vantage point, but Isabelle didn't press him. They could ask for directions once they were inside the camp. The guards helped them dismount, Margaret charming them in the process, as usual. Then they looped the reins around the hitching post, leaving enough slack so the horses could graze on the rich roadside grass.

They wandered through the lines of tents, searching for Ogilvy. Men were everywhere, sitting in the sunshine, whittling, cooking over small smoking fires, and cleaning their pistols.

"We could ask that one," Margaret said, clutching Isabelle's arm. Her customary sass seemed to have deserted her in this intensely male and rather primitive milieu. "Or what about the soldier over there? He looks friendly."

The soldier in question looked up from cleaning his broadsword and called out something in Gaelic accompanied by kissing noises. Isabelle recoiled. "I don't think so."

"They must assume we're trollops," Margaret whispered.

Heat suffused Isabelle's chest and rose up into her cheeks. It had been a mistake to come here; her natural caution had been overruled by her eagerness to solve the mystery of the salve. Recovering her nerve, she called out in ringing tones, "We are ladies. So treat us accordingly." The men burst into laughter, at least the ones who understood English. Others translated so all were in on the joke.

"Glad to hear it." A familiar figure emerged from between lines of tents. Rory MacGregor bowed. "Good afternoon, Lady Isabelle. Lady Margaret."

Isabelle experienced a rush of relief along with a springing joy she quickly squelched. "Good day, MacGregor. Take me to your master, please." At his frown, she clarified. "Lord Ogilvy."

He turned on his heel with a "come on" wave of his fingers. They scurried behind him as he wove his way across the camp.

Isabelle noticed that no one dared to stare at them or comment while he accompanied them.

"Lord Ogilvy, miladies." Rory bowed in front of a slightly larger tent with the flaps tied back.

At his invitation, they stepped inside. Lord Ogilvy sat at a writing table, scribbling a letter. A cot and several folding stools were the only other furnishings. Upon seeing them, he rose to his feet. "Good afternoon. How may I be of service?"

Broaching the subject of the salve right away seemed awkward, so Isabelle said, "This place is bigger than I imagined. If it hadn't been for your man, we would still be wandering around out there."

"My man?" Lord Ogilvy shot them a puzzled look.

"Rory MacGregor, my lord."

Lord Ogilvy burst out laughing. "Rory MacGregor? He is a laird in his own right." He waved at Rory, who was lingering outside and now stepped in. "MacGregor, I just learned that you serve me." He pointed to his shiny black boots. "Perhaps you could give these another polish."

Rory played along with a tug on his forelock. "Right away, milord."

Isabelle's cheeks flamed. "But I thought—when you came to my workshop, I assumed—"

"That I am Ogilvy's servant? That is understandable, so I forgive you." His eyes danced with merriment.

"Forgive me?" Isabelle clenched her fists in outrage and, she had to admit, embarrassment at her error. "A harmless mistake, was it not?"

Rory pretended to think this over, cupping his elbow with one hand while he scratched his chin with the other. "I suppose," he finally said. "As long as you address me as 'your lordship' from now on."

Isabelle jutted her chin. "I will not." She crossed her arms and glared.

Lord Ogilvy laughed. "This is all very amusing, but why don't you have a seat so you can argue in comfort?" He sat at his desk again, reaching a hand to touch the teapot sitting there. "This is still hot, if you would like a cup."

A soldier appeared outside the tent. "Lord MacGregor? You are needed."

"It appears my service is required elsewhere," Rory said. He bowed to Margaret and Isabelle, a smile still playing on his lips. "May I call upon you later today, Lady Isabelle? I have something to discuss."

Isabelle arranged her skirts and sat on one of the stools. "I may be at home. I am not certain." Her cheeks still stung with humiliation, and she wasn't quite ready to let Rory off the hook.

"I will make sure she is there when you call," Margaret said pertly. "Good to see you again, your lordship."

Isabelle feigned great interest in the cup of tea Ogilvy offered her, but inside she was squirming in discomfort. What did Rory MacGregor want with her? *Probably another prescription. What else?* To her surprise, this logical conclusion provoked a pang of disappointment.

"Did you have anything in particular you wished to see me about?" Ogilvy asked. "Not that I don't find your enchanting presence a nice distraction from the preparation of tedious dispatches."

Margaret glanced at Isabelle, waiting for her to take the lead. Isabelle stalled by taking another sip of tea. "Well, milord, I wanted to inquire about the effectiveness of my salve for your rheumatism."

"What service you provide." Ogilvy flexed one leg then the other. "I must say I am very pleased with it. The pain is much less, even on damp days when it acts up the most."

"I am so glad to hear that." Isabelle was also glad to know Rory had actually given Ogilvy the salve. Once again, her thoughts shied away from examining her emotions concerning the handsome Highlander too deeply.

"That is good news," Margaret said. "Especially since it can be so dangerous."

"Dangerous?" Ogilvy's brows rose. "What do you mean?"

Isabelle covertly stepped on Margaret's toe as a reproof. "What she means is that you should only use it twice a day at most and apply only a slight coating."

The nobleman nodded. "As I've been doing. MacGregor passed along your instructions to the letter."

"I thought I should check, since I didn't speak to you directly." Isabelle knew her pretext was thin, but perhaps he would swallow it. She changed the subject hastily. "I heard some unsettling rumors about the late Lord Lochmere. If they *are* false, perhaps you can squelch them. In the interests of morale."

"Oh my. That sounds quite serious." Ogilvy ran the feathered quill through his fingers over and over again.

"It is. He is said to have been a spy for the English," Margaret blurted.

"Lochmere? Never." Despite his protest, he didn't seem especially surprised at the accusation. "He did spend a lot of time wooing Whigs to our cause. Perhaps that is the rumor's source." He fell silent, staring into the distance sightlessly. "At least that is what he said he was doing. I didn't think much of Lochmere, to be honest. But Prince Charles would never hear a word against him." He put the pen aside and picked up the teapot. "More tea, ladies?"

"Lord MacGregor here to see you, Lady Isabelle."

Isabelle looked up from counting her bundles of dried herbs with relief. Rory hadn't given a time, and she'd idled away the afternoon with trivial tasks in order to occupy her mind.

"Send him up, please." After Nan nodded and left, Isabelle went to the small mirror to smooth her hair. Noting her anxious expression, she had to laugh. Why did she care so much about Rory MacGregor's opinion of her appearance?

Rory swept into the room, bringing with him his characteristic odor of wool, woodsmoke, and minty evergreen. Maybe even Highland soldiers used fragrance in their toilettes. "Lady Isabelle," he said with a bow. "I am glad to find you at home, as your cousin promised." His lips quirked in a smile.

Isabelle sniffed, refusing to respond to his teasing. "What did you want to talk to me about?"

His answer sent a thrill down her spine. "The tin you found in Lochmere's chamber."

Isabelle sank down upon a stool, her knees suddenly weak. The night of Lochmere's death, he had implied that he'd seen her furtive actions at the bedside, but she had thought she'd managed to put him off. Apparently she was wrong.

"What tin?" To her dismay, her voice shook. She clenched her jaw, annoyed at her weakness.

He sighed deeply and crossed his arms. "I saw the tin myself when we brought Lochmere into his chamber. I knocked it off the table with my elbow." He began to pace back and forth, able to take only a couple of steps in each direction in the small space. "Frankly, I thought nothing of it until I saw you pilfer it."

She seized upon a loophole. "How could I pilfer something that is my own?" She scrabbled around on the counter, found the object, and held it up between two fingers. "See? Wolfsbane salve for rheumatism, made by me."

Rory stopped dead and wagged a finger at her. "You cannot fob me off with semantics. I want to know why you took it back, if you gave it to him in the first place."

Isabelle bit her lip, her mind working furiously through her options and the likely outcome of each. She took a deep breath. *Can I trust him?* "All right. I will tell you. I think this salve killed Lochmere."

His eyes widened. "What are you saying? That he was poisoned?"

"Exactly. Either because someone gave him the wrong instructions or because they doctored it and made it much too strong." She reached up to the shelf and pulled down her remaining bottle of wolfsbane oil. "One of these is missing."

He stared at the oil, apparently speechless.

She seized the opening and went on the defensive. "Why are you questioning me, anyway? Did you suspect something wrong concerning Lochmere's death?"

Finally he tore his eyes away from the oil. "I cannot tell you that. All I can say is I was ordered to investigate any anomaly."

"And my actions qualified." Inwardly, Isabelle cursed herself. If only she had left the salve sitting there, it might have gone unnoticed. But instead she'd panicked. Maybe she could save the situation anyway, by offering her knowledge as a sign of good faith.

"I didn't prescribe that salve for Lord Lochmere," she said. "That is why its presence there concerns me. It was as if someone wanted me to be blamed." She picked up the oil again and set it down with a thump. "When I discovered the theft of my oil, I knew I was being implicated."

"Did someone steal the salve?"

"No." She pulled her ledger down from the shelf and flipped it open to the right page. "I keep an inventory of all the medicines I make and sell, especially those that can be dangerous. See?"

Rory ignored the ledger. "Who did you prescribe the salve to?" His brows rose. "Besides Ogilvy. That is why you went to see him today, is it not?"

She shrugged, trying to make light of it. "I was curious to see if he was still in possession of his salve."

Rory bared his teeth in a ferocious grin. "And that I wasn't the poisoner."

Ignoring his remark, she flipped the ledger shut and put it back on the shelf. "As I recall, I suggested the particular mixture. So you were never a suspect." That was true, but of course he could have decided to use it on Lochmere once he realized its potency. Then she had an idea, one that would help both of them. "Do you want to help me winnow my list? I need someone to go with me to the White Hart."

"Mr. Sloan certainly doesn't look like he needs liniment."

Isabelle had to agree with Rory's observation. The White Hart's landlord stood straight and strong as he moved about behind the bar serving customers, positioning casks, and lifting crates. He was younger than she had expected too, about five and twenty years, with long blond hair and broad cheekbones.

Rory took her arm. "Let's go talk to him."

She glanced around curiously as they wove their way through the bodies standing between them and the bar, noting the ancient tavern's beamed ceiling, creaky wood floor, and plaster walls stained yellow with age and smoke. The customers were mostly men of the laboring class with a couple of sailors and more than a few Highlanders mixed in.

Rory's wide shoulders made room for them at the bar. He tugged Isabelle forward to stand beside him. "I will have an ale," he said once he caught the landlord's eye. "What would you like, Lady Isabelle?"

"A glass of cider, please." It was bad enough that Lady Fenella's daughter was standing in a public house; she certainly wasn't about to drink ale or whiskey here. Or anywhere, actually. It wasn't ladylike.

The bartender served their drinks, Rory's with a foaming head of froth and hers in a small balloon glass. Rory paid him in coin. "Are you Mr. Sloan?"

The publican nodded. "Aye."

"Do you have a moment for a word?"

Sloan glanced around to check that no one needed his immediate services. Leaning forward on his hands, he said, "A minute, maybe. Go ahead."

Rory nodded at Isabelle before saying, "This is Lady Isabelle Ripa, the herbalist, and I am Lord Rory MacGregor."

Before coming in, they had agreed she would take the lead. Isabelle screwed up her courage and said, "We happened to be in the neighborhood, and I wanted to check on one of my prescriptions to see if it was satisfactory." She took in the man's unlined face and muscular arms and shoulders. "But I am guessing you are not the one who needed it since it was for rheumatism."

Sloan laughed and pointed at Rory's mug of ale. "That is the only prescription I need so far. Ale for what ails you, right?" He winked at Rory.

Playing along, Rory lifted his glass in a toast. "Good ales cure ails."

Isabelle was stumped. Dr. Donaldson had distinctly said the landlord of the White Hart. He must have lied to her.

"Perhaps you are talking about my father," Sloan said before she could go further with that line of thought. "The dear old codger suffered from terrible problems with his joints. Some concoction the doctor gave him did the trick." He shook his head. "May he rest in peace."

Rory gave Isabelle a significant glance. "My condolences."

Sloan sighed. "It was sudden. Lung trouble."

Isabelle stiffened. Was it pneumonia, which killed many an older person, or another case of poisoning? "I am so sorry to hear about your father." She paused. "Do you still have the medicine? I would like to take it back if so. It is not something anyone should use if not prescribed."

Rory jumped in. "It causes a nasty rash if misused. Leaves scars like smallpox." He patted his cheeks with a grimace. "All over your face."

Sloan's handsome face went white. Rory had got him where it hurt, in his vanity. "Let me check with my wife." He went barreling off, calling for Peg.

He was back in mere moments, shaking his head. "I'm sorry, Lady Isabelle. My missus says Doc Donaldson collected all of Father's medicine after he passed."

11

Creighton, Vermont
Present Day

Sofia was pulling the last pan of shortbread out of the oven when Donna Roberts, the official taster for the Best Biscuits company, appeared at the food truck window. "We've had a change of plan for the people's choice shortbread contest."

"What do you mean?" Sofia stared at the dozens of cookies she'd baked, all lined up neatly on cooling racks. Feeling the heat of the pan burn through her mitts, she hastily set it down on the stove top.

Donna compressed her lips. "There was a concern about fairness of the voting, so we're moving you all to the dinner tent."

"Are you afraid of ballot stuffing?" Vanessa asked, already back from her break. "We had that problem at prom. There were more votes than students."

"Something like that," Donna said vaguely, glancing at her ever-present clipboard. "You're table number two. Bring your cookies over in half an hour." With a wave, she hurried off.

"Does this mean we have to close the truck for the afternoon?" Wynter asked. "Bummer."

Sofia sagged back against the counter. "We have a bigger problem. How are we going to move all these cookies?"

The three of them stared at the tender golden disks in dismay. The cooling racks wouldn't work since the cookies would slide off. Because baked goods were best eaten fresh, she hadn't planned on saving leftovers, so she hadn't brought storage containers to the fair.

Vanessa snapped her fingers. "I have an idea. I'll borrow some clean boxes from the pizza stand. The biggest ones they have."

"Great idea." Sofia rummaged through her supplies. "And I've got a roll of parchment paper. We'll use that to line the boxes."

"And we can come back here and reload if we need to," Wynter said.

"I'll be right back," Vanessa called as she ran out the back door.

Sofia set the parchment paper on the counter. "Wynter, can you bring in the blackboard? And put the Closed sign up. We don't have much time."

Someone knocked at the back door and Sofia opened it, figuring it was Wynter lugging the sign. A middle-aged man in slacks and a short-sleeved shirt stood there, clipboard under his arm.

"Are you from the contest?" Sofia asked.

He flashed the ID hanging on a lanyard around his neck. "Bill Thompson. Health inspector for the fairground." Leaning forward, he craned his neck to peer inside. "Got a report of rodents."

"Rodents?" Sofia took a step back. "I haven't seen any rodents or any evidence of them." But Vanessa had seen a man carrying a mouse earlier that day. *Was he planning sabotage? Worse, had he succeeded?* Her stomach sank. A negative finding would be the kiss of death to her food truck license. And the Best Biscuits contest.

"May I take a look?" Bill put his foot on the step.

"Of course. But hurry, please. We have a contest to get to." She moved away from the door to let him in. Wynter appeared around the corner carrying the sign, and Sofia waved at her to stay outside.

Moving slowly as though giving the message that his inspection was more important than any contest, Bill climbed into the truck. Fortunately, most of the storage areas were empty. Sofia's supplies were in the refrigerator and freezer with a few dry goods stored in one cabinet. After checking the top cabinets, Bill got to his knees to peer into the floor-level ones. Vanessa joined Wynter outside, arms stacked with pizza boxes. Both were watching the proceedings anxiously. Sofia glanced at her phone. Less than fifteen minutes before the contest started.

Finally, with a shake of his head, the inspector scooted backward and rose to his feet. "I don't see a thing. You're clean." He made a notation on his clipboard.

At this announcement, Sofia flushed hot with anger. He'd wasted her time, and worse, someone had tried to get her in trouble. "Who filed the report? Obviously it was false."

"I can't say, ma'am. Confidential." He ambled toward the door. "Have a good day. Oh, and nice job keeping the place shipshape. Wish all of them were. Make my job easier."

Sofia flushed again, but this time it was with pride. She had set out to pass that inspection, and she had done it. Now it was on to the next challenge.

With only minutes to spare, Sofia and the girls made it to their station marked with a sign: 2—Sofia's Confectionery. Each of the contestants had his or her own long folding table in a row under the billowing white peaks of the open-sided tent. Sandy Wallace was on Sofia's right, in the first spot, and Annie Bowers of Granny's Green Mountain Bakery was on her left, at station three. At the end of the row, Donna sat at the voting table, a podium and microphone set up beside her.

Sofia placed the cooling racks along the length of her table, and the girls followed behind, unloading the boxes with gloved hands. She'd been asked to bake three gross, or 432 cookies. About half of them fit on the table, so they'd refill the racks as needed.

"Give over, ye wee beastie!" At the next table, Annie was struggling with the lid of one of her plastic storage containers, which appeared to be stuck. It suddenly let go and square shortbread cookies went flying everywhere, all over the table and onto the floor.

"Five minutes until the Best Shortbread Contest begins," Donna announced, her voice heard all over the midway through the public address system. "Anyone who wants to participate must line up at the food tent."

Annie dropped to her knees and began picking up cookies off the ground. Obviously, they were ruined. Sofia thought she heard the woman sobbing.

"Mom, why don't I go help her?" Wynter asked. "She's all alone."

Sofia's heart was touched by her young daughter's generosity. "Go ahead and ask if she wants your help."

At the questioning look Wynter aimed her way, Vanessa nodded. "Mom and I can handle this by ourselves. I'll hand out cookies, and Mom can load them up."

Wynter sidled over to Annie's table and bent down to talk to her. After a quick procession of confusion, doubt, and relief crossed the woman's face, she nodded. Wynter gave them a thumbs-up and started helping Annie set out her cookies.

On the midway, throngs of fairgoers milled around, obviously eager to take part in the contest. Donna stood at the podium again. "Hello, everyone. Welcome to the Best Biscuits Best Shortbread Contest." She paused to let everyone cheer. "This is the people's choice round. Four hundred thirty-two of you will be allowed into the tent by Sylvia." The fairgrounds office manager waved from her stool at the tent entrance, giving the crowd a big smile. "Participating in the contest means you will be giving consent to be filmed."

For the first time, Sofia noticed two camera operators stationed in the tent. Apparently Best Biscuits would be using this event in their marketing and publicity. "How do I look?" she whispered to Vanessa. "I didn't know I'd be on camera." Taking off a glove, she reached up to pat her thick waves into place.

Vanessa squinted and studied her mother. Taking off her own glove, she reached out and straightened Sofia's collar. "You look great. Maybe put on a little lipstick."

Sofia ducked down to root for her cosmetics bag in her purse. She quickly pulled out her lipstick and mirror and dabbed on a quick coat.

Donna continued with the contest instructions. "You will each move along the table to sample the cookies. Then at the end, you will elect your top four choices on this ballot."

Sofia tucked away her makeup and stood in time to see Donna pointing to a poster-size replica of the ballot. "After voting, you will put your ballot in this box." A wooden box with a slot in the top and a padlock securing the lid sat on the table. "Your top picks only, folks."

Sofia put on gloves and made a few last-minute tweaks to the arrangement of her cookies. *Please let my cookies be a top-four pick!*

"Three, two, one," Donna called. "The contest has now begun. May the best baker win!"

The crowd clapped and surged toward the entrance. "Brace yourself, Mom," Vanessa whispered. "Here they come."

The hour that followed was a blur of faces and smiles as fairgoers filed by, pausing to receive a cookie from Vanessa. Many commented on the cuteness of the dog design from Pat's cookie stamp, and Sofia hoped they were equally impressed with the taste. She could barely keep up with reloading the racks, and she was grateful that they had been able to bring the entire batch in one load. There simply wasn't time to go back to the food truck.

"How's it going?" Jim stood at the table, his arms around Luke and Matthew as he ushered them along.

"Good, I think," Sofia said. "Keep your fingers crossed."

"I'll vote for you, Mom," Matthew said loudly, drawing chuckles from people nearby. After Vanessa gave him a cookie, he ate with noisy praise.

"Let's have dinner here," Jim suggested. "They're having a wild hog barbecue."

"Wild hog?" Vanessa's face was horrified.

Jim laughed. "No, farm raised. But a nod to the traditional Highland boar hunt."

"Sounds good." Sofia was beat already, and she'd be up at first light again tomorrow to bake for the next day's customers. Not thinking about a dinner menu or preparations was a welcome break.

Jim and the boys continued on to the other tables, and Sofia noticed to her amusement that Matthew didn't greet the other shortbread offerings with the same enthusiasm he'd shown hers.

Finally, when she was about to drop, the last few people went through.

"Thanks for participating, everyone," Donna said over the PA system after they finished voting. "Results will be posted later." She directed a helper to grab the ballot box, and the camera operators started tearing down their equipment.

"I wonder how long we'll have to wait." Vanessa began to stack the empty racks.

"Hopefully not long." Sofia rubbed her lower back as she sank gratefully into one of the chairs behind the table. There wasn't any hurry to leave since she didn't have anywhere to be at the moment. Since they were out of inventory, she wouldn't be opening the food truck again until tomorrow.

Wynter bounced over to their table, apparently still full of energy. "I'm glad the fiddle players came. I bet their votes really helped."

"I hope so," Vanessa said. She nodded toward Sandy, who was busy packing up her table. "I saw an awful lot of *her* friends come through."

"How could you tell?" Sofia was curious about the possible hometown advantage for the local baker. No one at the games knew her, so she'd win only if she made the best shortbread, not because of loyalty. Though Vanessa's friend had said his fellow musicians would support her, she sincerely hoped they had all voted for their favorites. Of course, she also hoped hers was the favorite.

"I heard them call her by name." Vanessa brushed crumbs off the cloth using her hands. "Some even said they were going to vote for her."

Sofia noticed that Sandy had finished cleaning up her station and was preparing to leave. "Good luck, Sandy." Despite the woman's rudeness, good sportsmanship dictated that she be civil.

Sandy didn't bother to return the good wishes. Throwing Sofia a tight smile, she exited without a backward glance. *So much for civility.*

"Wow. That was rude." Vanessa scowled. Crouching down, she pulled the used pizza boxes out from under the table and stacked them by a nearby trash can to be recycled.

"She must be a bad sport," Wynter said. "Mom, I heard we're staying for dinner. What are we going to do until then?"

Before Sofia could answer, Annie came over to their table. "Thanks again, Wynter. Ye were a huge help, lassie."

"No problem." Wynter shrugged. "It was fun."

Sofia exchanged amused glances with Annie. Only a fifteen-year-old would consider the madhouse they'd just experienced "fun."

"How about we go get ice cream?" Vanessa asked. Wynter nodded eagerly at this idea.

"That's a great idea," Sofia said. "Look for Dad and the boys, okay? I'll be back at the food truck in a few minutes. You can all meet me there.

"I know I couldn't have handled the contest alone," Sofia said to Annie after the girls strolled off.

"Aye, that's for certain. The niece of a friend of mine was supposed to come help me. I can't imagine what happened to her." Annie peered down the midway. "I might speak to her aunt about it."

Sofia put two and two together. "Are you talking about Laura's niece?"

Annie's bright gaze was curious. "How on earth did ye know that?"

"My food truck is right next to her tent, and she mentioned her niece Mandy was helping out."

Annie snapped her fingers. "You took Madelaine's spot. The green truck." She shook her head. "What a bilious color. It's enough to put you off your feed."

Sofia laughed. Finally, someone who agreed with her. "You're right, it is hideous. Did you know Madelaine?" She seemed to be the only person at the fair who hadn't had the pleasure.

"Of course. My bakery is only the next town over and all of the pastry nuts know one another. Plus we attended a lot of the same fairs and events." She pursed her lips. "Sad thing, it was. A lassie half my age." Before Sofia could object to this obvious falsehood, Annie amended her remark. "Well, almost half my age. Two-thirds of it, more like. But still far too young."

They were silent for a moment, Sofia in acknowledgement of the woman's grief at losing a friend.

"She and Sandy Wallace used to be business partners," Annie said. "It wouldn't have been pretty if they'd both been in the contest today, I tell ye."

Sofia absorbed this new information.

"Madelaine was the better baker by far," Annie continued. "She had the touch."

Sofia shifted in her chair, uncomfortably aware that she was indulging in gossip. "What happened between them?" She imagined a dispute over money or direction or perhaps a personality clash. She knew from her own experience that Sandy wasn't the most agreeable person. What had it been like, working with her every day, especially in the hot and close confines of a bakery kitchen?

"Sandy inherited the bakery from her folks—they started it back in the '60s—but with Creighton's growth over the past few years, she realized she needed help. So, she hired Madelaine." Annie paused. "Then Madelaine ran off with Sandy's husband. That handsome devil Wendell MacKay."

12

Edinburgh, Scotland
September 1745

"At least we managed to scratch another patient off the list," Isabelle said glumly as she and Rory arrived back at her town house. "Lord Ogilvy and Mr. Sloan."

"That leaves the doctor and Lady Fiona?" Rory leaned against the balustrade, arms folded across his chest.

"That's right. The doctor outright lied to me. He said he didn't know how Mr. Sloan was doing." Isabelle snorted. "He is obviously doing very poorly since he is dead."

"I wonder why he felt the need to lie," Rory mused. "I will put some thought into how we can scrutinize him further. And Lady Fiona, of course."

"I appreciate your help in solving this vexing situation, Lord MacGregor, more than I can say." She choked a bit on the title, still feeling a fool over mistaking him for a servant. Now that she knew the truth, she couldn't imagine how she'd made such a blunder. His well-bred, confident manner marked him as a leader and a gentleman.

His grin was impudent. "You could call me Rory, but I believe you are the one who needs to suggest a first-name basis."

"All right, Rory it is. Please call me Isabelle." She put her hand on the latch. "Would you like to come in for a cup of tea?" Reluctant to let him go, she hoped he would say yes.

"Thank you, I think I will . . . Isabelle." He followed her inside and up the staircase to the living quarters on the second floor. The bottom floor was rented to a wool merchant, and Isabelle's family used the five upper floors.

"The drawing room is this way," she said, leading him along the cream-painted hallway hung with landscapes and ancestral portraits. At the doorway she halted, causing Rory to bump into her.

As if conjured by their words, Lady Fiona Ross sat cozily ensconced with Isabelle's father in matching wing chairs by the fire, tea service set out on a low table between them. Lady Fiona was pouring tea.

There goes my plan to discuss strategy with Rory over a quiet cup. Yet, it was an opportunity to learn more about the woman, both as suspect and as an unwanted admirer of her father. At least she hoped Lady Fiona's attentions were still unwelcome. Otherwise it might get tricky.

"Good afternoon, milady." Isabelle cast Rory a significant glance before moving into the room. "Hello, Papa." She made the introductions.

Lady Fiona's gleaming green eyes fastened on Rory with interest. "If men like you represent the Jacobite cause, I might have to change my views." Legendary as one of the most beautiful women in Edinburgh, today she shone in pale green watered silk that flattered her high-piled red hair and porcelain complexion. Tiny ruffles outlined her throat, upper chest, and wrists, bringing attention to their elegant structure.

Rory bowed over Lady Fiona's dainty hand. "I urge you to alter them for many more reasons than the poor example I present."

Lady Fiona cocked her head. "Very prettily said." She smiled at Isabelle's father. "Between the two of you, I am practically a convert."

Her father shook Rory's hand, then gestured to the fireside repast. "Please, join us." He and Rory pulled up a couple of armchairs to make a circle. The next few minutes were occupied with pouring additional cups of tea and passing plates of small crumpets.

"Tell me about your family, Rory," Lady Fiona said. "The MacGregors are from Glen Orchy, correct?" She took a delicate sip of tea, keeping her rapt gaze upon Rory.

Isabelle squirmed in her seat. She was curious to hear the answers to Lady Fiona's inquiries, but she didn't like the way the woman fastened onto Rory like a dog with a fresh bone despite the difference in their ages. Papa covertly wiggled his eyebrows at Isabelle and smiled, apparently amused—and relieved—that she had moved on to another conquest. If only she could share his relief.

"That is exactly right, milady," Rory said. "We still hold a small family seat there, even though ownership of our lands has often been disputed by other clans. In fact, we are still under proscription."

Isabelle gasped, then tried to cover her dismay by coughing. Didn't Rory realize how firmly Lady Fiona was on the side of England? Clan MacGregor had been almost eradicated a century ago. At times, use of the name was forbidden. Surely it was unwise to remind a possible enemy of his shaky legal status.

"So, you are practically an outlaw?" Lady Fiona's brows rose. "How intriguing." She extended her cup to Isabelle. "Fill me up again, if you would."

Isabelle decided a quick change of topic was in order. "Lady Fiona, how is the liniment I gave you?" Isabelle filled the teacup and handed it back. "I hope it has been effective."

Lady Fiona added a sugar lump to her tea and stirred before replying. "I am not sure what you mean." Her tone was cool, almost repressive. "I never use such things." She laughed, a brittle little tinkle. "I am in the very best of health, I assure you."

A flash of heat traveled through Isabelle, dampening her armpits. Had she made a dreadful mistake? Maybe Lady Fiona hadn't purchased the salve after all. Then she clearly conjured the entry on the ledger page in her mind: "Wolfsbane salve, Lady Fiona."

"I beg your pardon," she mumbled, refraining from pressing the matter in front of the others. Was Lady Fiona embarrassed about her illness, often an infirmity of age—or was her denial hiding something more sinister?

Holyrood's grand staircase is becoming almost as familiar as my own. With a sigh, Isabelle hoisted her skirts and began the long climb to the prince's apartments. Rory had mentioned that the prince held late-morning audience hours, and she hoped to get in to see him.

If it weren't for my formula being misused, you wouldn't get me anywhere near this powder keg of a situation, both literally and figuratively. She smiled at her own pun. "A wee bit of humor to sweeten the sour," as her friend Brenda would say. She'd awakened that morning with the unsettling but persistent notion that she should lay the situation before the prince. Her attempts to investigate covertly in hopes of keeping her name out of it had come to nothing. Perhaps meeting the problem head-on would bring better results.

Other petitioners filled the chairs in the Queen's Lobby. Due to the palace's disrepair, the prince used this wing for his chambers rather than the traditional King's Chambers. As Isabelle approached the secretary seated at the far end, she spotted a woman with three small children clustered about her knees, a soldier with a peg leg and eye patch, two stout merchants clutching invoices, and several noblemen doing their best to ignore the rabble.

"Name?" Mr. Murray, a middle-aged man with a high-arched nose and a supercilious tone, held his pen poised over the visitor list.

"Lady Isabelle Ripa." Despite her low volume, the words echoed in the high-ceilinged chamber, and she felt curious glances raking her back.

"Purpose of visit?"

She hadn't expected that question and certainly wasn't going to discuss the topic of Lord Lochmere's death in public. "I would rather not say. It is a private matter."

The woman with the children tittered, and Isabelle felt a blush sweep up her neck. "Not that kind of private," she hastened to clarify. "A business matter." That should satisfy since she did intend to discuss her herb dispensary.

"I will put business, then." He scratched the pen across the page. "Find yourself a seat, and I will call you."

The only open chair was beside the woman, unfortunately. As Isabelle arranged her skirts to sit, she heard her whisper, "Business, my foot."

Isabelle glanced at her smirking face before hastily turning away to study the ornamental plasterwork decorating the coffered ceiling. All the rooms in the palace were beautiful, and it was a shame they'd basically been abandoned. Her heart thrilled at the thought that when Prince Charles won, Holyrood would be returned to its former glory. Even if his sights were set on the monarchy of Britain, surely Edinburgh would still be an important seat of power in tribute to the Scots who risked all to boost him to the throne. Especially men like Rory, whose lives depended upon remaining invisible to the English.

A stab of anxiety clenched her stomach. *I am going to meet Bonnie Prince Charlie, the future King of England.* To cool her heated cheeks, she waved a hand in front of her face. Then she remembered the calming lavender oil she usually kept on her person and dug the vial out of her reticule. Uncapping it, she inhaled deeply. Almost immediately she felt the soothing scent settle her nerves.

"What's that in your hand?" the woman whispered.

"Lavender oil, for the vapors."

The woman scoffed. "Likes of me never get the vapors." Her none-too-clean hand reached for the vial. "But let me try it."

Isabelle allowed her to take the bottle and watched in amusement as she inhaled, once hesitantly and then with vigor. The woman's eyes widened. "Och. That smells so sweet." She let each child sniff the oil in turn.

"Lady Isabelle Ripa," Mr. Murray called, followed by rustling and grumbles as the others waiting realized she had somehow skipped the line.

Isabelle hastily retrieved the oil, capped it, and thrust the vial back into the woman's hands. "You may keep it—in the event you should need it," she said with a sweet smile.

No time for nerves. She twitched her skirts into place and scurried down the long room toward the door to the inner chamber, now held open by a guard. She nodded at him and went through, then stopped short, her head bowed.

"Lady Isabelle Ripa," the guard said. The door clicked shut.

"You may approach."

Isabelle raised her head. The prince sat behind a desk instead of on a throne as she had imagined. As on previous occasions, she was struck by the contradiction between his youth and the invisible mantle of authority he wore so lightly upon his narrow shoulders. Was he born to a royal demeanor or did it result from the constant deference of others?

Realizing she was staring, she moved across the carpet to

what she considered a suitable distance and curtsied deeply. "Your Royal Highness."

"You may rise."

She straightened and again found her attention caught by his personage. Every thought about why she was here fled out of her head. Perhaps guessing that, he nudged, quite kindly. "Why did you wish to see me?"

"Sorry. Yes, Your Majesty." She dug in her reticule and pulled out the tin of salve she found at Lochmere's bedside. "I wanted to show you this."

He held out his hand and she moved close enough to drop it into his palm. "I found this in Lord Lochmere's room. You can see the tin is marked as made by me. The problem is, I did not prescribe it for him, and if used wrongly, it is poisonous."

The prince was nothing if not insightful. "You believe Lochmere may have been murdered?"

"Yes. I spoke to Dr. Donaldson, and Lord Lochmere showed no prior symptoms of a heart malady. To clinch the matter, someone stole a bottle of the formula's most toxic ingredient from my workroom."

The prince leaned back in his chair and regarded her through narrowed lids. "You are Fenella MacDonald's daughter, correct? If not for her reputation, I might think you had something to do with it."

Isabelle swallowed, her throat suddenly dry. She needed to tread lightly or she might find herself in a cell before nightfall. "It is because of my family's loyalty that I approach you, Your Highness. I could have hidden the tin, and no one would have been the wiser." *Except the killer, of course.* "Certain things I have heard bolster my belief that Lord Lochmere did indeed die before his time."

He tossed the tin into the air and caught it with one hand. "And what, pray tell, did you hear?"

She straightened her shoulders. "I heard he might be a spy for the English."

His gaze went to the guard. "Leave us."

Isabelle's knees began to shake. What was going to happen now? Surely if she were in trouble, he would have sent for more guards, not dismissed the one. But somehow that notion didn't stop the quaking.

After the door swung shut, the prince did something totally unexpected. He smiled and asked, "Do you like to dance, Lady Isabelle?"

"Let me get this straight. Prince Charlie recruited you to his service this afternoon?" Margaret waved her hand-painted Jacobite fan in agitation. "And this happened how?" She and Isabelle were in the carriage, on their way to another ball at Holyrood.

Isabelle didn't blame Margaret for her skepticism. She still couldn't believe it herself. "As I said, he asked me if I liked to dance, which seemed a rather strange inquiry considering our topic of discussion."

"Lochmere's death."

"That's right." Isabelle's innards quivered as she uttered the startling news once again. "He confirmed that Lochmere was indeed suspected of being a spy."

"The rumors were true, then."

"Apparently. They were on the verge of arresting him for treason when he died. Naturally, Prince Charles let the matter go. 'No point in hanging a dead man.'" She shivered. "Those were his exact words."

"But now Lochmere's brother has arrived."

"Yes. William, the new Lord Lochmere. And I have been deputized to discover which way he truly leans." How she would manage to do that was still a mystery to her. She certainly wasn't a skilled seductress, able to force men to confess their innermost secrets with a wave of her fan. Bonnie Prince Charlie probably should have chosen Margaret.

Her cousin pooh-poohed the idea when she said as much. "I am too indiscreet. Besides, you are incredibly lovely in that moss green. You will melt every man's heart tonight."

"You really think so?" Isabelle smoothed her velvet skirt, which was inset with a cream brocade underskirt and trimmed with ivory lace panels. While she hoped her appearance tonight was appealing, it wasn't the new Lord Lochmere she hoped to impress. Rory MacGregor was earning a larger share of her thoughts than he deserved. The day before, he had excused himself from tea well before the tiresome Lady Fiona had. Isabelle hadn't seen or heard from him since. She hoped to discuss with him Lady Fiona's denial regarding the salve as well as the next steps in the investigation, but obviously she couldn't depend on Rory MacGregor; hence, her visit to the prince.

Margaret sighed. "Do you suppose he is handsome?"

"William, you mean?" Isabelle thought of the late lord's doughy face and portly build with a shudder. "Let's hope he is more well-favored than his brother."

To her delight, their friends Brenda and Allan were standing inside the Great Gallery handing out the memento fans. Seeing that Margaret had brought hers along, Allan handed one to Isabelle with a flourish. "A keepsake, Lady Isabelle."

"Thank you, Allan." Isabelle opened the ivory-handled fan so that the painting was fully displayed, a fanciful depiction of the prince as a Roman emperor surrounded by cherubs. She fanned herself, enjoying the cool breeze upon her face. "I will treasure it always."

Margaret briefly rested her half-open fan against her lips. "Remember, this means you want a kiss."

Isabelle swiped at her with the fan. "And this means you are a cheeky minx." After they stopped laughing, she thought of something. *How on earth am I going to identify William, let alone find him in the heaving throng of men and women milling about the ballroom?* Maybe Brenda and Allan could describe him.

"I heard that William, the new Lord Lochmere, has arrived," she said. "Have you seen him?"

Brenda's brow creased. "Have we, Allan? So many people have passed by, it is all a blur."

Allan rubbed his chin. "I think so. He is accompanying Lord Lovat." He put his hand up to indicate a man's height. "Very tall, wearing Fraser dress tartan like mine and a black velvet evening coat."

Brenda's face lit up. "Och, the good-looking one? How could I forget him?" At Allan's doleful expression, she gave his arm a squeeze. "Not for me, silly. For these girls. They are not lucky enough to be engaged to a fine gent like you."

Margaret gave Isabelle the "kiss me" gesture with her fan again and winked. "We will be on the lookout."

One thing about plaid, Isabelle mused as they strolled the length of the ballroom, *is that it makes identifying people a wee bit easier.* That was, until the numerous bright tartans and their variations became a confusing jumble in her brain.

She collapsed into one of the gilt side chairs. "I give up, Margaret." Half an hour into her first royal assignment and she was a failure.

Margaret sat beside her with a sigh. "There are far too many people here. With our luck, as we walked up one side, he was going down the other."

The orchestra struck a tune, and when couples formed squares for the first quadrille, Isabelle had an idea. She could sit here in comfort and watch the dancers for William.

Margaret had the same thought. "Let's see if we can spy him on the dance floor." She glanced at the drink table nearby. "Perhaps we can convince someone to bring us punch." Opening her fan, she waved it fetchingly while searching those around them for a friendly face. Her ploy worked. Within minutes, a young man in Campbell tartan detached himself from a group and made his way over to them. Although not exactly handsome, he had a friendly, freckled face and twinkling green eyes. He wore his auburn hair tied back in a queue rather than tucked under a powdered wig, as many of the nobles did.

"Lord Harry Campbell, at your service, miladies." He bowed and clicked his heels together—an unnecessary but nice touch, Isabelle thought.

After shooting Isabelle a triumphant glance, Margaret held out a languid hand. "Nice to meet you, Lord Campbell. I am Lady Margaret MacDonald and this is my cousin and best friend, Lady Isabelle Ripa. Would you be so kind as to bring us each a cup of punch?"

"I'd be glad to, milady. Wait where you are." He dashed off to the drink table, kilt flying in his wake.

"I think he is smitten," Isabelle said. "Nice work."

Margaret watched Harry as he ladled two cups of punch, eyeing the levels carefully. "There *is* something very appealing about him. He looks like he would be good fun."

Harry returned in short order and handed them each a cup of punch. At Margaret's invitation, he sat beside her and was soon regaling them with humorous tales of his travels from the

Highlands. Although obviously educated and intelligent, he affected the manner of a simple country lad who found city life surprising and rather alarming.

Isabelle was so entertained, she was startled when the orchestra stopped and bagpipes proclaimed the prince's arrival at the ball. Everyone stood respectfully as the guard shouted, "His Majesty, Prince of Wales!" People on both sides of the room moved back against the walls to let him pass.

From where she stood, Isabelle couldn't get a good look at the prince or the couple following him into the room. But she clearly heard the guard's announcement of their identity.

"Lady Fiona Ross and Lord Rory MacGregor."

13

Creighton, Vermont
Present Day

Luke nudged Sofia with an elbow. "Are you going to eat that, Mom?"

Sofia looked at her half-full plate of "wild hog" barbecue. Although the pork, roasted potatoes, and green salad were tasty, she wasn't able to eat much. The results of the contest still hadn't been announced, and her stomach was knotted in anticipation.

She handed Luke the plate. "Go ahead and finish it, if you want."

"My son, the bottomless pit." Jim reached over and ruffled Luke's hair.

"You're one to talk," Sofia said. "Isn't that your second piece of apple pie?"

"Guilty as charged." Jim grinned and cut off another bite with his fork.

The big tent was filled with families enjoying the pit-roasted pork dinner while listening to a well-known fiddler and cello duo playing Celtic favorites. Tamping down her impatience, Sofia forced herself to really concentrate on the sweetly piercing music, so evocative of heather-covered hills in a land far away. *Is it possible that Isabelle once listened to these very songs? Music is a timeless thread through the centuries, binding us all in a shared experience.*

Lost in fanciful thoughts, she didn't notice Donna enter the tent. She was startled to see her take the stage when the duo took a break. One of the camera operators followed, setting up the tripod and a light stand at one side.

"Here it comes, Mom," Vanessa called from the next table, where she and Wynter sat with the young fiddlers.

"Don't worry, Alice and Jeremy will be right back," Donna said into the microphone. "But now it's time to announce the results of today's shortbread contest, the people's choice round. Going for the top four, folks." She paused until the audience's rustling and chatter quieted. "Number four, Ross Bakery." Modest clapping followed. On the other side of the tent, Sofia saw the couple bob to their feet for a bow.

"Number three. Granny's Green Mountain Bakery." There was a round of slightly louder clapping for Annie.

Wynter raised both hands in a victory clasp. "I helped her win!"

The knot in Sofia's stomach was now a boulder. If she wasn't named one or two, then she was out. Why hadn't she checked out her competitors? She had no idea where she ranked regarding the other shortbread since she hadn't tasted anything they baked.

Donna paused, making the crowd—or at least the remaining contestants—suffer. Finally, she leaned forward and spoke. "Number two is Wallace Treats. That's your local bakery, folks." The tent erupted, affirming that Sandy was well-known to many attendees.

Sofia scuffed her shoes back and forth in the dirt under the table, unable to sit still. If she lost, then of course she could stay on at the games and sell baked goods and research the family tree. Wasn't that the original reason they had come here anyway? She tried to comfort herself with these reasonable thoughts but failed miserably. In anticipation of losing, she closed her eyes and wondered if it would be too childish to put fingers in her ears.

"I've got all my eyes, fingers, and toes crossed." She opened her eyes a crack to see her wonderful husband holding both hands up, eyes squinted and face screwed up in anticipation.

She laughed. "Thanks, honey. You're the best."

The atmosphere in the tent was thick as Donna wrung every drop of tension from the buildup to the winner. Finally, when Sofia was about to scream, Donna let the other shoe drop. "And the winner of the people's choice award is . . . Sofia's Confectionery."

There was dead silence for a long moment, then the teen fiddlers jumped up in unison with a roar of approval. Their hoots, cheers, and whistles spurred a huge round of applause. At Jim's urging, Sofia stood for a bow, causing the noise level to rise even further.

As the acclaim swelled, Sofia found herself raising her hands in a victory salute like Wynter's, relief and gratitude making her lightheaded with joy. She had done it. Her shortbread recipe had made the first cut. She was still in the running for the big prize.

Across the sea of people, Sofia caught a glimpse of Sandy Wallace, an acidic smile pasted upon her face.

Jim dropped Sofia at the food truck at six the next morning to prepare the day's supply of baked goods, then brought the rest of the family to the fairgrounds at eight. The girls helped her set up while the boys and Jim went to an archery lesson. At ten, Sofia would attend Dr. Campbell's lecture.

At a quarter before ten, Julie's cheerful face peered through the food truck's window. "Knock-knock. Anyone home?"

Marla appeared beside her. "I saw you on TV last night, Sofia. Congrats." She smiled at Wynter and Vanessa. "You must be really proud of your mom."

"We are," Vanessa said. Wynter echoed Vanessa as she offered Julie and Marla each a lemon tart.

"Wow. This is stellar." Julie ate hers in two bites.

Sofia pulled off her apron. "Girls, we're going to see Dr. Campbell, and then we'll be back to take over."

Wynter pirouetted, almost hitting her sister with one outflung arm. "Great. I can't wait to go to the Highland dance lessons."

"Me neither," Vanessa said. "Mom, did you pack my helmet?" She gave her sister a smirk.

"Be good, you two." Sofia grabbed her purse out of the broom closet, checking to be sure she had the picture of the quilt square to show the clan expert. Then she joined her friends outside for the walk over to the exhibit hall located at one end of the midway.

"I've never been to a Highland Games," Marla said, gazing around at the booths and carts. "Look at that lovely tartan." She pointed to Laura's tent where lengths of softly colored plaid were displayed on racks. Laura sat at a spinning wheel, working the foot treadle as her hands guided the wool. She gave them a brief wave of greeting.

"I haven't even had a chance to shop," Sofia said. "I've been so busy baking."

Julie paused at a display of silver jewelry. "You haven't been shopping? For shame." She pointed at the leather booth. "Oh, boots to die for." With a nod to the proprietor, she added, "Definitely to die for." She gave Marla a nudge.

Inside the booth, Wendell MacKay was shining a tall brown boot with a cloth. In addition to footwear, a variety of bags, packs, belts, and vests were for sale. Sofia regarded Wendell with mixed feelings. He was undeniably attractive, but what she knew of his romantic history made her uneasy.

Julie had no such compunction and practically dragged Marla over to the booth. "What nice things. Did you make them?" She picked up an embossed leather belt and studied it. "Mark would love this."

Wendell smiled. "I make everything except the footwear." He set the boot down with a chuckle. "We have long winters here in Vermont." He noticed Sofia standing off to one side. "Congratulations on winning yesterday. You deserved it."

Sofia felt a wave of warmth at Wendell's flattery. "Thanks. I hope I'll survive the next round tomorrow." She began to poke around the display of wallets, thinking she might buy one for Jim. Standing next to them on the table was a small pill bottle from Bluebell Farm. This one read, "Male Over-40 Boost." Did Laura supply all her friends with supplements?

"Sofia's a great baker," Julie said to Wendell. "We love everything she makes."

Wendell began to polish the boot again. "I take it these are friends of yours?"

Before Sofia could answer, Julie jumped in. "We sure are. I'm Julie and this is Marla." She tugged Marla forward, a matchmaker with a reluctant client.

"Nice to meet you," Wendell said. "So, are you ladies attending the big Highland Ball tomorrow night?"

"You didn't tell me about the ball, Sofia," Julie said. "I'll see if Mark wants to come over for it. I know there's no room for him at the cabin so we'll go home after." Julie's husband, an engineer, was Jim's good friend.

"No fair. I don't have a date." Marla crossed her arms and pouted, half in jest. A widow for ten years, she had begun to date again, but she wasn't ready to look for a serious relationship.

"I'll take you," Wendell said. "I don't have anyone to go with either." His gaze was somber.

Julie squealed and clutched Marla's arm. "Oh, say yes! We'll have so much fun."

"All right. I mean, thank you, yes." Marla looked pleased at the idea of a date with the handsome Wendell.

Sofia bit her tongue. She could fill in the others about his romantic history later. "We'd better get going. Dr. Campbell's presentation starts in five minutes."

"We'll talk about arrangements later, Marla. Have a good day, ladies." With a final smile, Wendell bent to his task.

Outside the booth, Julie squealed again. "I'm so excited about the ball. I assume we're to dress in Highland costume?"

"We'll have to figure that out after the lecture," Sofia said. Feeling eyes on her back, she turned to see Laura glaring at them from her seat behind her spinning wheel. *How strange.*

Marla patted her handbag. "That reminds me. I got some genealogy information on Isabelle from my contact."

"Let's look at it later," Sofia said as they approached the door of the exhibit hall. "We'd better hurry, or we'll be late for the presentation."

Dr. Campbell, dressed in a green-and-blue tartan kilt signifying his clan, was a burly older man with a thick gray beard and a gravelly voice. His talk was on the Scottish clans, their history, movements, and relationship to each other, complete with maps and diagrams projected on a screen. Sofia was riveted.

"A watershed moment for the clans was the arrival of Bonnie Prince Charlie in Edinburgh in 1745." Dr. Campbell pressed the control and a portrait of the handsome young prince flashed onto the screen.

Julie raised her brows. "And your ancestor was right in the middle of it," she whispered.

The realization that an ancestor was connected to one of history's most intriguing people filled Sofia with awe. What a rich legacy Nonna had left their family.

He went on to detail the banning of the plaid and the clearing of the Highlands that followed the upstart's decisive defeat at the hands of the English. But he ended on a hopeful note, saying that the emigration of the Highlanders spread their culture and way of life to new places, including all of New England and the Appalachian Mountains.

After the talk concluded, Sofia and her friends waited until the room cleared out before approaching Dr. Campbell, who was packing his laptop. "Hi, I'm Sofia Parker. We have an appointment."

He slid his computer into its case. "That's right, we do." He gestured at the chairs nearby. "Why don't we stay right here?"

Once they all settled down, Sofia handed him a photo of the tartan quilt swatch, explaining her inheritance of the quilt and diary. "We thought this looked like a MacGregor tartan."

Dr. Campbell stroked his beard as he considered the photo. "I think you're right. Of course, my opinion isn't entirely conclusive since I don't have the actual fabric." He waved the paper. "What's your connection to the MacGregors?"

Sofia glanced at Marla, who pulled out the papers regarding Isabelle. "Sofia's ancestor, Isabelle Caroline Ripa, lived in Edinburgh in 1745. At least that's what the diary says. Birth records show that she was born in Edinburgh in 1727. Her mother was Fenella MacDonald, a rather famous beauty, I gather."

"And?" Dr. Campbell's thick, caterpillar-like eyebrows rose.

"We're not sure," Sofia said. "The diary says Rory MacGregor wore that tartan. But we haven't found more of a connection between them than that."

"And we haven't found any further records of her. No marriage or death certificates."

"You have me curious now." Dr. Campbell pulled a small notebook out of his chest pocket and jotted a note. "I'll take a look in my records regarding the 1745 Jacobite Uprising. Perhaps we can find out what happened to your Mr. MacGregor."

"Thank you, Dr. Campbell." She hoped he would be able to shed light on the mystery of Isabelle's life. "I do have one other question." At his inquiring look, she said, "My husband's mother was a Gregg. Someone mentioned that the Greggs were part of Clan MacGregor. But his family came to the United States in the early 1700s and settled in New Hampshire. Nutfield, his mother told him. Do you think they're connected?"

The professor nodded. "Remember when I spoke about the Scots-Irish in my lecture? They weren't actually Irish; they were Scots who emigrated to Ireland. A branch of the Gregg family did that and were among the first to come over here for new opportunities."

"That's fascinating." Sofia took her own notes. "I can't wait to tell my husband."

Dr. Campbell pushed on the arms of his chair and stood, his signal that the meeting was over. "You're a lucky woman to have MacGregors in your family on both sides. They're a clan known for their independence and bravery. '*S Rioghal Mo Dhream*. 'Royal Is My Race.'"

"Wow. Royalty." Julie made a mock curtsy toward Sofia. "Should we address you as Your Highness?"

Sofia rolled her eyes at her friend's teasing. "You can if you want, but I won't answer."

After leaving the exhibit hall, they strolled down the midway, back to the food truck, discussing the lecture and preparations for the ball. "It's settled," Julie said. "I'll run back to Cabot Falls in the morning and pick up dresses and shoes for you two. Then I'll come back with Mark in time for dinner."

"I'm glad we women only need to wear a tartan sash with black dresses," Marla said. "I really can't afford a ball gown right now." She clutched a bag holding three silk sashes in the MacGregor modern red tartan.

"I hear you," Sofia said. "Buying Jim a full formal Highland outfit would cost a lot of money." Now she had to convince him to go to the shop to buy the kilt, hose, shirt, jabot, and shoes. The jacket could be rented, much like a tux rental.

As they walked past Annie's food truck, the tantalizing scent of meat pies drifted their way.

Julie took a big sniff. "I'm starving."

"Me too," Marla said. "Isn't it almost lunchtime?"

"The owner is one of the shortbread contestants," Sofia said. "Let's go check out her wares."

But as they drew closer, Sofia spotted something troubling. Annie was standing outside the truck, arguing with Bill, the health inspector.

"Ye can't close me down!" Annie yelled, her accent growing stronger. "It's no' fair that ye do such a thing! I'm in the contest, ye see."

14

Edinburgh, Scotland
September 1745

For a moment, the ballroom swam with a haze of noise and light. Isabelle thought she might faint. She swayed on her feet but fought the profound temptation to sit. Such a breach of protocol was unacceptable at court.

Margaret clutched Isabelle's forearm. "Did he say what I thought he said?"

Isabelle leaned gratefully on her cousin's shoulder. "I am afraid so." The appearance of Lady Fiona at a Jacobite function was unexpected, but Rory escorting her was the real shock. Perhaps it was innocent; maybe he had simply won her over to the cause. The strength of her reaction made her realize something: She cared far too much about where the Highlander placed his affections.

The prince ascended the dais at the end of the room and gestured for everyone to be at ease. "I hate to interrupt the merriment with another of my boring speeches so I won't be keeping you from the dancing for long. However, we do have a small piece of business to attend to." He grinned. "A very gratifying one, I must say."

Rory and Lady Fiona approached the dais. Rory bowed. "Your Majesty, may I present Lady Fiona Ross, your loyal subject."

Lady Fiona moved forward and knelt on the floor. "I wish to give the oath, Your Majesty."

A wave of mutters went through the room as the revelers realized what was happening. The prince stepped off the dais and stood close enough to Lady Fiona to touch her, should he wish.

"This is truly astonishing," Margaret whispered, fanning herself vigorously. "A Ross has never sworn fealty to the Stuart cause. Her support is a significant victory for the prince."

"Her vast fortune will also be welcome," Harry said.

Margaret rolled her eyes and snapped her fan shut. "Trust a man to be pragmatic."

His reply was immediate and to the point. "How else can we provide for our ladies?"

"Hush, you two." Isabelle strained on tiptoe to see around several large figures blocking her view of the proceedings. Following along with Rory's prompts, the noblewoman gave the oath, her hands clasped as if in prayer.

"I gratefully accept your allegiance, Lady Fiona, and wish you long life and good health," the monarch said. "Please rise." Holding out his hand, he helped her up, to the cheers and jubilation of the observers. "Let the music begin," he said, still clasping her hand. The musicians struck up a waltz, and the couple swept around the floor, Lady Fiona's gold brocade skirts belling out as she followed the prince's masterful lead. Years at the French court apparently had honed his agility on the ballroom floor, along with his other courtly skills.

"That lucky woman . . . dancing with the prince . . ." Margaret's sigh was wistful.

"Will I suffice as a poor second?" Harry asked, a hopeful look in his hazel eyes.

Margaret tapped her closed fan to her lips as she pretended to consider. "I think you will do nicely."

Harry beamed. "Now it is *my* lucky day." He put an arm around Margaret's waist, and they joined the couples spinning about the floor.

Isabelle stood off to the side, feeling conspicuous as the crowd around her thinned. Her hopes that Rory would ask her to dance were dashed when he whirled by with an elegant matron in his arms.

"May I have this dance, milady?" Lord Ogilvy asked with a bow.

"Of course." *Released from being a pitiful wallflower at last.* No matter how many balls she attended, she never quite got over the fear that she would be ignored and overlooked. Every time a man asked her to dance, she felt a small charge of relief.

"You are looking lovely tonight, Lady Isabelle." Although Ogilvy was slight in build and a tad shorter than Isabelle, he steered her about the floor with vigor and determination.

"Thank you kindly, Lord Ogilvy. I find you rather dashing yourself." The older man was indeed dapper in his gray evening coat, white lace ascot, and silver-embroidered blue waistcoat.

"Your prescription is working a treat," Ogilvy said. "I can move freely and without pain." As though to demonstrate, he twirled her even faster.

"I am so glad to hear that, milord." Satisfaction warmed Isabelle's heart at this news. His appreciation reminded her why she had become a healer: to restore her patients' health and enjoyment of life.

They danced past Harry and Margaret, so engrossed in each other that they didn't notice Isabelle. *There's a marriage in the near future there, I'll wager.* She was glad for her cousin. Someone as warmhearted as Margaret deserved true love and an honorable man. Harry fairly radiated goodwill and kindness.

Ogilvy nodded his head. "Did you hear about the new Lord Lochmere coming to court?"

Isabelle followed his gaze to a tall man in a black coat and Campbell kilt, his hair hidden by a powdered wig. Brenda was right. He was very attractive indeed—in fact, one of the best-looking men in the room. A tiny thrill hummed in her veins. If she was required to operate as an agent of the throne, at least her quarry was intriguing.

"I would appreciate an introduction," she said, "so I can welcome him to the cause."

Ogilvy threw back his head and laughed. "That can be arranged, my dear young lady." He leaned close, dropping his voice to a whisper. "I have the feeling Lord MacGregor better step lively if he wishes to declare himself."

Isabelle's cheeks burned. "I am not quite sure what you mean, Lord Ogilvy." Was he implying that Rory was interested in her? And were her feelings for him so obvious? *Oh, horrors!*

"Oh, I think you do, Lady Isabelle." His eyes twinkled mischievously.

Lord Ogilvy was as good as his word. When the dance ended, he parked Isabelle at her chair and soon brought William over to meet her.

William bowed over Isabelle's hand. "I am delighted to make your acquaintance, Lady Isabelle. If I had known the ladies of Edinburgh were so fair, I would have journeyed here long before now." Upon closer examination, he was even more handsome, and so different from his brother in demeanor that it was hard to believe they were related.

"You flatter me, milord. Welcome to our city."

Margaret and Harry arrived in a whirlwind of high spirits and good cheer. Upon catching sight of William, Margaret threw Isabelle a saucy wink. "I see you have reeled in your fish," she whispered.

After Ogilvy excused himself, the two couples took to the dance floor. As William led her away, Isabelle spotted Rory headed toward them. Their eyes met and he frowned briefly before smoothing out his expression again. With a curt nod, he stopped to talk to someone else, giving the impression that this had been his plan all along.

The minuet made conversation difficult since couples moved apart and together in a series of stylized steps. The entire time, Isabelle racked her brain as to how to broach the topic of loyalty with William. She couldn't blurt out questions. She should work around to the topic gradually.

When the intricate and tiring dance ended, Isabelle opened her fan and waved it vigorously. "I am finding it close and crowded in here. I could surely use some air." She smiled winsomely, feeling entirely false and certain he would see through her ruse.

By some miracle, he accepted her flirtatious act. He bowed. "Let me escort you to the courtyard."

They moved side by side through the long ballroom and down the grand staircase in company with other couples seeking privacy on the pretext of needing fresh air. When she spotted Rory standing on the lower landing in close discussion with Ogilvy and two other men, she thought at first to pass by without acknowledgment. Then she realized that would be a huge breach of manners.

"Good evening, Lord MacGregor." By using this address, she was signaling that they should remain formal, here in company.

"And to you, Lady Isabelle." Rory extended a hand to William. "I don't believe we've met."

The men exchanged greetings and pleasantries while Isabelle hovered nearby. Beyond one questioning glance, Rory made a point of ignoring her. She returned the favor, feigning great interest in the conversation.

"If you will excuse us, the lady would like to take some air," William finally said. As they moved down the staircase again, Isabelle felt Rory's glare like a dagger between her shoulder blades. Although she held herself rigid, inside her thoughts were churning. She longed to turn to him and scream, "How dare you bring Lady Fiona to the ball? And then act like a churl when I talk to another man?" Of course he didn't know she was on a mission for the prince, unless the monarch had told him. But Prince Charles had sworn her to secrecy, saying, "Two people can keep a secret, but only if one is dead." He was right. While she had already disregarded his wishes by confiding in Margaret, who would certainly never tell a soul, it wouldn't do to compound her error. She had trusted Rory with her own secrets, but the confidence of the prince was an entirely different matter.

The inner courtyard was bordered by a colonnade that allowed strollers to remain sheltered while enjoying a view of the gardens, now in a state of neglect like the rest of the palace. A lamppost in the center of the expanse shed barely enough light for Isabelle to see her companion's face as he walked beside her, hands clasped behind his back.

"Have you been in Edinburgh long?" she asked, deciding that was an innocuous way to begin.

"I arrived yesterday, the soonest I could get here after hearing the news about my brother." His tone was somber.

"I am so sorry for your loss," she murmured. "It was so very sudden."

"The sentiment is appreciated, milady."

In the cover of dusk, she found she could focus on his voice, not only the words but also the tone and inflection. As a consequence, she had the distinct impression that he didn't exactly mourn his brother's death. Was he yet another person who had wanted the elder Lochmere dead? He certainly benefited since he now held the title.

Had he poisoned his brother? If so, how had he managed it at a distance? Did he have an accomplice in Edinburgh?

Distracted by her thoughts, Isabelle lost her footing and tripped on a paving stone.

"Careful, milady." William gripped her elbow with a firm

hand, steadying her. "You might fall." The heat of his fingers burned through the delicate fabric.

Isabelle's heart raced at his touch, at the unwelcome idea that she might be alone in the dark with a killer. To her great relief, she spotted Rory and Lady Fiona coming along the colonnade from the other direction.

"So we meet again!" she called gaily, waving her hand.

Rory's eyes widened at her exuberant greeting, in such contrast to her earlier manner, but he merely nodded. Lady Fiona was much more enthusiastic. She unfolded her fan and waved it vigorously despite the rather cool evening air. "And who is this, pray tell? Introduce me, Lady Isabelle." Her coquettish smile was fetching, and William immediately responded.

Feeling rather as if she were delivering yet another romantic morsel to the rapacious noblewoman, Isabelle made the introductions.

"Oh, I see," Lady Fiona said. "You are here because of the unfortunate demise of your sibling."

"That is not the only reason, milady." He began walking again and the others followed suit, Lady Fiona by his side, Rory and Isabelle behind them. "I have other matters to attend to while I am here in the city."

What matters? Isabelle's ears pricked up. She held her breath, hoping to hear something she could take to the prince. Then Rory put a detaining hand on her arm, allowing the other two to draw some distance ahead.

"What exactly are your intentions with this act, Isabelle?"

His harsh tone made Isabelle jump. Had he figured out she was working for the prince and disapproved? Or was his anger due to something else entirely? Jealousy, perhaps? A ray of hope warmed her heart. "I am simply taking a turn around the garden with a gentleman. That is all." *All you need to know about it, that is.*

In the meager lamplight, his dark shining eyes sought hers. "Are you certain? He doesn't . . . mean anything to you, does he?"

"How could he? We just met." With a sudden spurt of annoyance, she put her hands on her hips. "Besides, what do you have to say about it? You accompanied Lady Fiona tonight." She peered down the portico at the other couple, who were conversing as they sauntered along. The peal of Lady Fiona's laugh echoed along the enclosure. "We should go. Your partner will wonder what you are up to."

In response, Rory took her elbow and drew her into an alcove, out of view. "This is what I am up to," he said roughly.

The kiss took Isabelle by surprise. For a moment she stiffened, not sure if she should protest. But his lips were warm and gently insistent, and gradually she allowed herself to relax into his embrace, to lean against his broad chest and revel in the strong arms encircling her. She'd enjoyed kisses before, but none so utterly consuming, so gorgeously transcendent, as if Rory and she were merely two halves of a whole.

Hearts and souls meeting in a kiss . . . The fanciful thought made her spirit soar like a falcon.

"Where do you suppose they went?" Lady Fiona's tone was querulous.

Rory released Isabelle with a rueful grin. "I suppose we'd better join them." He ran a hand along her cheek. "We'll talk later."

Isabelle hastily pushed her hair into place as they stepped back into the main walkway, certain the other couple would guess what they had been doing.

"Sorry we lingered behind," Rory said smoothly as the other couple approached. "Isabelle was giving me advice about an ailment one of my men is suffering."

Isabelle played along. "As I told Lord MacGregor, I see many cases of grippe in the autumn. My formula should do the trick," she added to Rory with curt professionalism.

"Are you an herbalist, Lady Isabelle?" William asked. "I am impressed."

"One of the finest in Edinburgh," Rory said. "All the nobles consult with her. Isn't that so, Lady Fiona?"

"I suppose so." Lady Fiona's green eyes flitted around as if discussing Isabelle's work was of very little interest. "Who is ready to dance? I would like to." Without further ado, she took Rory's arm and fairly dragged him along the passage. "Are you coming?" she called back to Isabelle and William.

Isabelle and William followed more slowly. She could scarcely think about anything but Rory. Their kiss, still fresh on her lips, made her stomach swoop and her cheeks tingle with warmth. For the first time, she understood what it meant to be "walking on air." She even peeked down at her slippers to make sure they were still touching the paving stones.

"I am quite interested in healing plants," William said. "At home we of course grow our own. Our old housekeeper fancied herself a healer, and I used to follow her around to learn her secrets."

Isabelle forced herself to pay attention so she could fulfill her promise to the prince. Once she had, she could turn her attention to more personal matters such as Rory and his kisses. "We have a wonderful physic garden here in Edinburgh, not far from Holyrood as a matter of fact. You really should visit it—if you have time, of course."

"I'd love to see it, Lady Isabelle. But on one condition—that you give me a tour."

"I doubt even this warm milk and honey will help me sleep," Margaret said. She and Isabelle were curled up on Isabelle's big bed, dressed in flowing white nightgowns and chatting before turning in. Margaret frequently stayed over after they attended social events together.

Isabelle laughed. "I know what you mean. My mind is awhirl with everything that happened tonight." She still glowed from the memory of Rory's kiss. But rather than discuss that, she said, "I take it you enjoyed Harry Campbell's company."

Margaret's smile was dreamy. "Oh yes. He is wonderful. How can it be? You meet dozens of men and then there is one who is simply perfect."

"I know what you mean." Isabelle couldn't help it; she had to say something to relieve the pressure fizzing through her chest like cider.

"Have you been holding out on me, Isabelle?" Margaret gave her a mock scowl. "I thought I was your favorite cousin."

"Oh, Margaret, you are much more than that." She took a deep breath. "Rory kissed me tonight."

Margaret shrieked, causing her hand to lurch and spill milk onto the silk counterpane. "Oops! Sorry! I am so happy, I forgot myself."

"Don't worry about it." Isabelle found a handkerchief and mopped at the spot.

Margaret set the mug on the nightstand. "I had better put this down before I really make a mess."

"You approve?" Isabelle asked.

"Approve? I'm elated. He is magnificent." She clasped Isabelle's arm. "Tell me all the details, and spare nothing!"

Isabelle told her how they ended up meeting in the courtyard and about his unexpected embrace. "I really thought he was enamored of Lady Fiona. That's when I realized that—"

"You cared." Margaret clapped her hands in triumph. "How perfect. What happens now? Are you seeing him again?"

A sliver of unease pierced Isabelle's haze of happiness. "I'm not certain. After we went upstairs, he excused himself for a meeting with the prince." She thought back to his manner when he kissed her hand in farewell. She believed she had seen an unspoken message in his eyes, but maybe she was wrong. Had she been a mere diversion?

"Oh, Margaret. I hope I haven't been a fool!"

"I doubt it. I've seen the way he looks at you."

"I wish I could be as certain as you." She decided to change the subject. "I do have a social engagement with William tomorrow. We're going to the physic garden."

"My goodness, you're quite the butterfly. William is also a fine specimen, for certain." Margaret grinned. "Perhaps I should drop a word to Rory . . . make him jealous."

"That's not why I'm going, and you know it." Isabelle wagged a finger at her cousin. "It's my assignment."

"I wouldn't mind an assignment like that," Margaret sighed. With a roll of her eyes, she clutched at the neck of her nightgown like a lovesick maiden.

"Stop it. You know that Harry is the only one for you."

"You're right. I was only teasing." Margaret adjusted her expression into a semblance of solemnity. "Did you learn anything about William?"

Isabelle shook her head. "Not much. We were interrupted when Lady Fiona and Rory came along." She took a sip of milk and set her mug beside Margaret's. "But I did get the impression that he doesn't exactly mourn his brother's death."

"Who did?" was Margaret's tart reply. "I have not met a single person who liked him."

"True. I hate to say it, but I wonder if we should consider William a suspect."

Margaret sucked in a breath. "Really? Why?"

"Because he benefitted from Lochmere's death. Now he has the title and all the family wealth."

"How could he kill him long distance from his home?"

Isabelle shrugged. "That's the puzzling part. Unless he has an accomplice here." Something William had said tickled at the back of her mind. "He did say he was interested in healing plants, so he probably has some knowledge of wolfsbane and its properties."

"This situation keeps getting more convoluted. Whom can we trust?"

"The only two people I'm absolutely sure of are sitting in this room, I'm afraid."

15

Creighton, Vermont
Present Day

"I'm sorry, ma'am." Bill, the health inspector, made a note on his clipboard. "It's out of my hands. You're closed as of now." With a glance at his watch, he jotted down the time.

Annie harrumphed and turned on her heel, headed toward the door of her truck. Then she spotted Sofia and changed direction. "Sofia. The fools have shut me down!"

Sofia discreetly told Marla and Julie to go on without her as she put a comforting arm around Annie and led her aside.

"What happened?" Sofia asked. Surely an experienced baker like Annie knew how to follow the food safety rules.

Glancing around, Annie lowered her voice. "He said he found evidence of mice." She clenched her fists. "I don't see how. I follow all the procedures."

A chill ran down Sofia's spine. If Vanessa hadn't intercepted the workman, would she, too, have been shut down? "I suppose this means you can't bake in that truck for the contest."

"That's right, worse luck. I might as well pack up, go home, and pray no one gets wind of this. It could ruin me."

"You can't bake in *that* truck," Sofia said again.

"That's what I said." Annie gave Sofia a funny look.

"But you can bake in my truck. Why don't you come over tomorrow morning with fresh supplies and your recipe? We only have to make a dozen cookies for the local panel round."

Annie put her hand on Sofia's arm. "You'd do that for me?"

"Why not?" Sofia took a deep breath. Should she confide in the other baker? Perhaps forewarned would be forearmed. "You know, something odd happened to me yesterday." She told Annie about Vanessa's experience and the surprise health inspection made on her truck because of an anonymous tip.

"You think we're being sabotaged." Annie's face was grim. "I'd better not find out who's behind it. It won't be pretty."

"What's on the agenda for tonight?" Sofia asked Jim after everyone convened at the food truck to discuss possible plans.

"I thought we'd have a picnic here at the fairgrounds," Jim said. "Brian is competing in the caber toss finals in a few minutes."

"And we've got the haggis hurl right after," Luke said. "Me and Matthew."

"Real haggis?" Julie's lip curled. "Isn't that sheep stomach?"

Luke laughed. "No, it's just a beanbag."

"Too bad, huh? Otherwise it would explode everywhere." Matthew made explosion sounds, complete with gestures, to Wynter's disgust.

"Can we watch the fiddling contest at six?" Vanessa asked. "It's the finals and Justin made it."

"Absolutely," Sofia said. The fiddlers had been her best supporters in the shortbread contest. It was her turn to cheer them on in the outdoor grandstand.

As Sofia locked the truck, Jim plotted their course. The events they wanted to attend were in relative proximity, so they would be able to make them all. First on the list was the caber toss. They met Brian Sinclair outside the fenced-in contest area. After greeting everyone, he turned to the kids. "I need someone to take care of the dogs for me. Do you think you can do that?" They eagerly agreed. Wynter took one lead and Matthew the other, since it was his turn.

"What exactly is the caber toss?" Julie asked him.

"See those poles?" He pointed to a pile of long skinned logs, almost the length of telephone poles. "We pick 'em up and toss 'em."

"Wow," Sofia said, eyeing the heavy posts. "I'll bet you'll work up an appetite doing that. You better join us for dinner."

He nodded, giving Marla a sidewise glance. "I'd like to, thanks."

Julie elbowed her friend after he walked away. "Who knew there were so many eligible bachelors here?"

"I know, right?" Marla's smile was wry.

A large crowd gathered for the caber toss finals. From what Sofia overheard, it was one of the games' signature events. It was certainly amazing to watch the men pick up the huge logs, trudge forward, and fling them. They weren't ranked on distance, but were judged on the log's controlled end-over-end flight and landing position. More than one man jumped away as the heavy pole came sailing back toward his head, the audience crying out in dismay.

Laura walked up to their group as Wendell strolled onto the field.

"My money's on Wendell," Laura said. "He may not be bulky like the other guys, but he's rugged." She curled her arm, making a muscle.

"You hear that, Marla?" Julie teased. "Your date is strong. Hopefully he's a good dancer too." At Laura's puzzled look, Julie clarified, "Wendell is taking Marla to the Highland Ball."

"What are you talking about?" Laura's mouth dropped open in confusion, but when her eyes met Sofia's, she closed it firmly and sidled away from them, down along the fence to another spot.

Had Laura been hoping he would ask her? That theory certainly fits with her proprietary attitude and the glares she gave us earlier when we were talking to him.

Wendell took his position and picked up the massive caber with the assistance of two helpers, then trotted forward across the grass. As Laura had promised, Wendell's throw was nearly perfect despite his apparent lack of brute strength.

While the spectators cheered, Sofia noticed Brian staring at Wendell, jaw set and face red with what appeared to be anger toward his rival. It seemed he was channeling all his grief and pain over Madelaine when he hefted his caber and charged forward with a roar. His throw matched Wendell's in form and grace.

Several men conferred and measured them. "It's a tie," the judge called through a bullhorn. "A runoff between Wendell MacKay and Brian Sinclair."

Both men were sweating and breathing hard, still tired from the previous throw. To roars and whistles, they stepped forward to throw the massive cabers again.

"Watching this makes me want to break out the weight set," Jim whispered in Sofia's ear.

She took his firm bicep and squeezed. "You get plenty of exercise splitting and stacking our firewood."

"That's true. They say it warms you twice—once when you split it and again when you burn it."

The tiebreaker throws were close, and the judges conferred silently as the crowd waited breathlessly. Finally, one of the judges spoke privately to the emcee who then addressed the crowd.

"For the third year in a row, Brian Sinclair is the caber toss champion!" Brian silently accepted the medal the judge hung around his neck before trudging across the grass and through the gate to join the Parkers.

The boys and Jim surrounded Brian with questions and praise, but Sofia's eye was caught by a scene a short distance away. The much shorter Laura stood on tiptoe, yelling at Wendell, her fists clenched. Sofia watched in horrified surprise as Laura reached up and slapped him across the face.

She glanced at Marla, who was busy laughing at something the boys were saying. Was it a good idea for her friend to attend the ball with Wendell? "Complicated" seemed to be a good description of all his relationships.

A couple of hours later, after they dined on fried chicken and potato salad during the fiddling contest, Sofia still hadn't decided what to say, if anything. Wynter and Vanessa were practicing their Highland jigs on the grass nearby while Jim, Brian, and the boys went for a walk with the dogs. The children had been beside themselves when Brian offered Fergus to the family and Jim and Sofia agreed to take him.

The three women were relaxing with a glass of wine, enjoying the warm evening while watching the sun sink behind the nearby hills.

"When you go to my house, get my black pumps," Marla said to Julie. "Wendell's tall, so I can wear those for a change." She turned to Sofia. "My last date, an insurance salesman, was so short I could see the bald spot on his head. From above!" She burst into infectious giggles, joined by the others.

"Speaking of Wendell, here he comes now." Julie pointed her chin to the back of the lawn. The tall bagpiper was winding his way through the families seated on blankets and in folding chairs. He wore a T-shirt and ordinary jeans instead of a kilt, and his hair was still damp from a shower.

"I like him better in a kilt," Julie said. "But he's not half bad dressed down."

Marla blushed. "You're so awful, Julie. Shhh. Here he comes."

Wendell gave them a wave as he approached. "Mind if I join you?"

"Of course not." Marla scooted over on her blanket to make room, her face flaming even more brightly.

"Would you like a glass of wine?" Julie held the bottle up.

"Don't mind if I do." He made himself comfortable, legs crossed and arms resting on his knees. He took the plastic cup of white wine Julie handed him, and they all sat in silence for a moment.

"That was an exciting competition earlier," Sofia said to get the conversation rolling.

"Yeah, it was." Wendell rolled his shoulders. "I'm still sore."

"I don't see how you guys can do that," Marla said. "Those cabers are huge."

"It's all in the wrists." Wendell chuckled. He gave Marla a sidewise glance. "I'm sorry about that ugly scene afterward."

"I don't know what—" Marla began.

"You mean with Laura?" Sofia cut in.

Wendell's face was sheepish. "Yes, with Laura. Anyway, I've come to release you from my invitation, if you want, Marla. You're nice, but I think I got ahead of myself." He cleared his throat. "You see, my girlfriend, Madelaine, died unexpectedly a couple of weeks ago. She was a baker, like Sofia. In fact, Sofia is using the truck she rented."

Marla and Julie made noises of distress. "I'm so sorry," Marla said, patting his knee. "I didn't know." She shot Sofia a frown.

"I was going to tell you," Sofia mouthed.

"I don't want you to get the wrong idea. I'm not anywhere near ready to date, of course. But I have to attend the ball as head bagpiper, so I thought you might—"

"Say no more." Marla's tone was firm. "We're friends, that's all. And yes, I still want to go." Behind his bent head, she rolled her eyes at Julie and Sofia, making a moue of disappointment.

"Thanks for understanding." His head still bent, Wendell plucked at the grass. "If only I'd been here, she might not have died."

Sofia asked, "Why do you say that, Wendell? How could you have prevented a heart attack?"

He shrugged broad shoulders. "Maybe not prevent it . . . but help her after? It took a while for the ambulance to get here, I heard." He picked up his cup and took a sip. "I tried to get her to come to the games in Connecticut that weekend, but she said she felt like she was coming down with the flu." His expression was anguished. "Do you think it was coming on and we didn't know?"

"Many women don't show any symptoms at all," Julie said briskly. "You can't blame yourself." She pointed at her friends. "That's why you should get regular checkups."

"Yes, Mom," Marla muttered.

"So, the whole gang was out of town except Madelaine?" Sofia asked. *Poor thing. She was all alone.* She shivered at the idea of falling ill with no family or friends nearby.

"I think so." Then his brow creased. "Actually, no. Brian was here." His lips quirked briefly. "Which meant I won the caber toss that weekend."

16

Edinburgh, Scotland
September 1745

The morning after the ball, Isabelle dragged Culpeper's *Complete Herbal* off the shelf. Although the wolfsbane salve was highly effective, she was in search of a new liniment recipe.

I can't in good conscience use a recipe that has killed someone. Especially one administered with that purpose in mind. From now on, she would use no poisons in anything she made.

Developing a recipe took her hours. First she decided how the medicine was to be administered—in liquid, pill, or ointment form. She found ointments to be the best for aliments of the joints, since the very act of rubbing in the mixture seemed to soothe the pain.

To complicate matters, the herbals were mainly a compendium of herbs, with very few full recipes listed, so she was required to create her own blends. That took thought, deciphering, and deliberation, as well as an experiment or two.

As she pulled licorice root, dried cayenne peppers, and nettle juice from the shelves, she was thankful for one thing: Her work calmed her mind, quieting the churning thoughts about Lochmere's death, her spying assignment, and the more pleasant but still troubling subject of Rory MacGregor.

"I have an idea." Margaret's voice boomed from the doorway, making Isabelle jump and almost drop the bottle of nettle tincture.

"Margaret, please. You have a bad habit of barging in with no warning. Can't you see I'm working?"

Her cousin glanced at the herbs lining the counter. "I promise I'll only be a minute. Why don't Harry and I go to the gardens with you and William today? I know you are worried about seeing him alone."

"That's true, but I do need to gain his confidence. And I can't do that with you two listening in, I'm afraid."

Margaret snapped her fingers. "I know. We will go to the gardens and watch you from a distance. But you will have to stay in full view the entire time."

Isabelle found a compounding bowl on the shelf. "Not a problem, I assure you." She looked at her ingredients, considering. "Since you're here, can you do me a little favor?"

"Certainly, I have a few minutes. Then I'm going home to get ready for Harry."

"Can you go down to the kitchen and ask the cook for a pound of hog grease? I need it to make my new salve."

The disgust on Margaret's face was comical.

The physic garden was located near Holyrood Palace, so Isabelle rode her mare down the Royal Mile to meet William. She thought that after viewing the herb beds, they could take a turn around Holyrood Park, a picturesque route that would lead them past St. Margaret's Loch, the peak Arthur's Seat, and several quarries. Surely at some point during all that, she would be able to determine his political state of mind.

"Good afternoon, Lady Isabelle." Mounted on a bay stallion,

Lord William Lochmere came alongside her as she approached the palace. Today he wore a kilt, a black coat, and a black cap with a feather. No white cockade, she noticed with disappointment.

"How are you, Lord Lochmere? It's a fine day for a ride." The dry, warm weather continued to linger, and it was pleasant to be out-of-doors.

"That it is." He pointed a gloved hand at the hump of Arthur's Seat in the near distance. "I'd like to get a closer look at that peak after we tour the gardens, if you have time."

"Exactly what I was thinking." Isabelle slid off her mount before he could assist her and tied the reins to the hitching post. "The garden is only a short way from here." She waited while he tied his horse, and then she led the way along the graveled path to the gardens, a series of rectangular beds built in the shelter of Holyrood Abbey.

"How long has the garden been here?" William asked.

Isabelle thought for a moment. "About seventy years. Doctors Balfour and Sibbald built it in 1670." She thrilled with pride at the advanced learning her home city exemplified. "It was one of the first botanical gardens in Britain."

The beds were arranged in historical order, the first showcasing herbs used in the days of the ancient Greeks. William made a most satisfactory companion as they peered at and discussed each plant.

"'Hart's tongue fern. Used for snakebite.'" He read the label affixed to the drying fronds. "I will have to remember that."

"Fascinating, isn't it? There appear to be herbs and plants to cure every human ill under the sun."

A black-robed figure strode their way, and Isabelle recognized Dr. Donaldson. "Good afternoon, Doctor."

The doctor barely gave Isabelle a grunt of greeting, keeping his eyes fixed on William instead. "How nice to see you again, William. How is your mother?"

Isabelle started in surprise upon realizing that Dr. Donaldson already knew William. Crouching down to examine a Christmas rose's buds, her ears went on high alert.

"She is fine, doctor. Thank you for asking." No doubt realizing the rudeness of their exclusive conversation, William said, "Lady Isabelle, Dr. Donaldson is my mother's cousin. I've know him since I was . . . what, about this high?" He demonstrated.

"I believe so. You were a cunning little towhead; that much I remember." Dr. Donaldson laughed, a rare action that totally transformed his face from dour gloom to something almost handsome.

Speculation ran wild in Isabelle's mind. Could Lochmere's death be a plot between the doctor and William, perhaps at the behest of William's mother? As the trio strolled along the path, the two men chatted about mutual acquaintances in William's hometown of Perth, a city about fifty miles away.

Isabelle noticed Margaret and Harry arriving at the gardens. As planned, they stayed within view but didn't approach. In addition, she thought she saw Lady Fiona arrive at the main gate of Holyrood Palace in her carriage. The ancient palace and its grounds were quite the social gathering spot, it appeared.

"When are you going to take the oath, my dear lad?" Dr. Donaldson put his hand on William's arm, his face intent with urgency. "We need you in this fight."

Isabelle wished she could chime in on the prince's behalf, but she refrained in the interest of discretion.

William sighed deeply. "I wish I could give you an answer now, my friend. I assure you I am giving your request full consideration. However, the responsibility for my estate lies upon my shoulders now, and I have dependents to consider."

The doctor's face blanched. "Are you saying that you believe our sovereign will lose? I can scarcely believe my ears." He glanced toward the castle as if afraid that someone of the prince's cabinet or the monarch himself might overhear this treacherous talk.

William's lips set in a stubborn line. "I think nothing of the sort. But I don't take oaths lightly, and I will not be pressured into doing so now." Tilting his chin, he gazed steadily at the doctor, apparently unfazed by the risk of taking an unpopular position—unpopular in Scotland right now, at any rate.

Dr. Donaldson's pale cheeks flushed. "You are a far different man than your late brother, I'll give you that." He snorted. "I half believe his loyalty was expedient at best, a way to escape his troubles here."

For a moment, Isabelle thought William might defend his brother. Instead, he said, "My brother was no friend of mine or my mother's, as you well know. However, I don't wish to speak ill of the dead."

Donaldson seemed to realize that he had gone too far, for he bowed and apologized, then made his excuses and moved away.

"My apologies," William said, his eyes still on the doctor's retreating figure. "I suppose such speculation is inevitable. Everyone loves to pick over a carcass."

"I take it you and your brother weren't close," Isabelle said, slightly worried that she might fall into that obnoxious category. "Is that because he was so much older than you?" She began to walk slowly toward the next garden bed, William keeping step with her.

"That's a large part of it. We had different mothers, you see. When my father died, we moved back to my mother's family holdings in Perth. We weren't welcome at Castle Lochmere, I gather. I was only an infant at the time; I only know what I've been told."

"It's sad you lost your father so young. I lost my mother too." Isabelle brought the conversation back to herself so as not to make him feel she was probing into his personal background.

After touring the rest of the garden while conversing amiably, they circled back to the horses. Margaret and Harry still lingered, sitting close together on a bench nearby. Isabelle waved and threw them a smile. At their evident enjoyment of each other's company, she moved up her predicted announcement of an engagement by a month or two.

"Do you still want to go for a ride, William?" Isabelle asked.

"I'm game if you are." William cupped his hands to help her mount. "I love nothing more than a good canter on a brisk autumn day."

Isabelle laughed in agreement as she stepped up into her sidesaddle. "Nor do I." To her alarm, the moment she settled her weight into the saddle, the horse bolted at full speed down the path.

Unprepared for the horse's lurch forward, Isabelle almost toppled backward onto the ground. Only her right leg wrapped around the pommel prevented her from falling. Using all her strength, she regained her balance and hunkered low over the mare's neck as she galloped into the park.

"Whoa, girl. Whoa!" Isabelle tugged on the reins—not too hard, as her groom taught her, but enough to signal "stop." But both verbal and physical cues went unheeded. The mare rocketed down the graveled lane as though shot from a cannon, hooves thudding. The passing woods blurred into green, and Isabelle had to squint against the wind that was making her eyes water.

What am I to do? Ride until the poor thing drops dead? She'd owned the horse for several years and the mare had always been biddable and docile. *Something must be wrong.*

Reaching a fork in the path, the horse went right along a narrow, winding route below the quarry cliffs. Panic clutched Isabelle's belly. A misstep here meant a tumble down the steep hillside. Now and then a hoof hit a patch of loose rocks, sending them clattering down into the gully. At any moment her mount could slip and they'd tumble, a fall that would likely be fatal, either by being thrown or by the crushing weight of the horse landing on top of her.

The wind rushed in her ears. The pounding of the mare's hooves was a constant drumming. Her world shrank to a pinpoint as she held on for dear life and prayed she would survive this wild ride.

But then she felt a stronger vibration, slightly out of sync with her horse. Could it be another rider approaching?

Incoherent sounds crystallized into shouts. "Hang on, Isabelle! Hang on!" Hope flared. Maybe she would survive this after all. Instinctively, she managed to nudge the mare closer to the cliff to make room on the narrow path. Within seconds, another horse came alongside. Gathering her nerve, Isabelle tore her eyes from the road ahead and glanced over at the other rider.

Rory MacGregor. His face was a mask of determination as he urged his black stallion to move faster, to edge ahead of her horse. By some miracle, he latched onto the bridle. Using the superior weight of the larger horse, he forced her horse to a trot, then a walk, and finally to a standstill.

As soon as it was safe, Isabelle slid from the horse, almost collapsing in the road as her knees gave way. Rory reached her in time to catch her. He pulled her roughly into his arms. "Oh my dear, oh my dear," he mumbled over and over into her hair. She could feel him trembling.

She was trembling too, out of shock and relief. "You saved my life. I really thought we were going to go over any moment."

He pulled back, placing both hands on her shoulders. "Frankly, I thought so too. The path gets worse up ahead. There were some rockfalls, and the debris hasn't been cleared away."

At the mental picture his words created, Isabelle's stomach flipped over and she clutched her midsection, thinking she might vomit right there. Seeing her distress, Rory led her to a large boulder beside the path. "Sit, please." He found a flask of water in his saddlebag and gave it to her to drink. She took a few sips and found the cool liquid settled her stomach.

"What happened?" he asked.

"I don't know. She took off for no reason I could see."

"Nothing startled her?"

Isabelle shook her head. "No. It was so very strange. She's generally a very agreeable creature. I usually have to kick her hard to make her run."

Rory went over to her mare and began to unlace the strap.

"What are you doing?"

"Something made her bolt." He pulled off the saddle.

"Where did you come from, anyway?" She glanced down the path. "And I wonder where William is. He must have thought I was insane to take off like that."

He rested the saddle on a large rock. "In answer to your first question, I was coming along a side path when I saw you race by. I could tell you were in danger so I came after you." He tugged off the horse blanket. "As for Lord William, I have not seen him today."

Hoofbeats thumped in the distance. It was only a moment before several riders came around the bend. William, Margaret, and Harry.

"Oh, Isabelle, you're all right! I was so worried!" Margaret slid off her horse and ran to embrace her cousin.

"Glad to see you're in one piece," Harry said, dismounting.

"At first I thought you were playing some kind of game," William admitted, "but these two convinced me otherwise."

"You didn't say 'race,' did you?" At Isabelle's headshake, Margaret smiled grimly. "See, I told you. That horse startled for some reason."

William's eyes widened in horror. "I am so sorry, Isabelle. Please forgive me."

Isabelle waved his apology away. "It wasn't your fault." However, it was fortunate that Rory quickly grasped the nature of the emergency. Her admiration for him grew even more.

Harry joined Rory, who was studying the underside of the horse blanket. "Did you find something?"

"I'm afraid so." Rory held up a small brown object between two fingers. "Isabelle's mare had a burr under her blanket—literally."

Isabelle staggered to her feet as the meaning of his words sank in. The horse had been in pain, attempting to flee from the sharp thorns stabbing into her hide. *But she was fine earlier . . .*

"That must have been placed there deliberately!" Margaret was outraged. "Who could have done such a thing? You might have been killed, Isabelle."

"You think someone did it on purpose?" William sounded doubtful. "Maybe it was attached to the blanket and the groom didn't notice it."

Isabelle found her voice. "Then why didn't she react sooner? She was fine on the way to the gardens." She shook her head vehemently. "My groom would have noticed. He's very meticulous."

"If this is someone's idea of a joke, then it is certainly in very poor taste," Harry said. He patted Isabelle on the shoulder. "I'm glad you're all right."

"Me too." Margaret threw her arms around Isabelle again.

When Rory's eyes met hers, Isabelle knew what he was thinking. She was getting too close to the truth about the elder Lochmere's death. Unfortunately, she was no closer to learning who was responsible. Until then, she was obviously in danger.

A shaken Isabelle returned home to find a summons from the prince waiting, written on thick vellum sealed with his insignia. He wanted a report on William, she knew, although the missive was brief and merely asked her to come to Holyrood within the hour.

"Shall I send an answer, milady?" Nan asked.

"No, I need to go there now." She glanced at her wrinkled riding habit. "Well, after I change. Please have the coach brought around." She wasn't going to ride the mare for a while, if ever again, although she supposed that was a cowardly attitude. The poor creature did need time to recover from several deep puncture wounds, and maybe she'd recover from her aversion by then.

Isabelle started to climb the stairs to her chamber but then paused. "Please let the cook know we're having three guests for dinner. If she can make a beef roast, that would be perfect." Harry, Margaret, and Rory were coming over that evening for an impromptu dinner party. She had invited William, but he was dining at Lady Fiona's. "We'll eat in the dining room. Oh, and please come up in five minutes to lace me up."

"Very good, milady." The maid whisked away to the rear staircase, accessed through a door at the end of the main hallway.

Once in her chamber, Isabelle stripped off her riding habit, put on a fresh shift, and washed her face in the basin. Under better circumstances, she'd have a full bath before visiting the monarch, but there really wasn't time. According to Rory, he was attending a council meeting that evening.

What am I going to tell His Highness about William? The dear boy doesn't realize what a mess he'll be in if the prince suspects him of treason. She needed to measure her words carefully—tell the truth but refrain from slanting it either way.

Isabelle forced herself to concentrate on choosing a dress and submitting to Nan's vigorous lacing of her corset. The finely woven gold wool would serve well enough for her meeting and also dinner with friends, she figured. After the maid fixed her hair and Isabelle powdered her face, she grabbed a shawl and draped it around her shoulders.

"I'll be back in an hour or so." *I hope.* She was eager to have the ordeal over. Perhaps he would release her from further spying duties.

"Yes ma'am." The maid tittered as she held the bedroom door open for Isabelle to pass. "Who would believe my mistress would be invited to call upon our future king?"

"It is rather startling, is it not?" Isabelle hid a smile. The maid would be startled indeed if she knew the true nature of the prince's summons.

17

Creighton, Vermont
Present Day

"Thanks again for letting me work in your truck," Annie said as Sofia unlocked the food truck. She clutched a box of baking supplies and pans in both arms.

"No problem," Sofia said as they entered the truck. Once they were inside, she closed the door firmly to keep out mice and the man who carried them around in his pocket.

Sofia pulled sticks of butter out of the refrigerator to soften. "Let's talk about these attempts to sabotage us." She moved around the space, gathering her baking equipment. "Did a workman come to your truck yesterday?"

"Yes. Someone from the fairgrounds crew came by to check the electrical service. In fact, he made me leave while he looked around. He said he was testing the draw on the circuits."

Their eyes met. "I'll bet he's the same man who came here," Sofia said. "One of the other contestants is trying to make sure we don't win."

Annie's grin was fiendish. "Well, it hasn't worked yet."

Sofia put on a CD of Celtic harp music and they worked on their cookie batches for a while, each lost in her own thoughts. Sofia wasn't going to bake for customers today since she needed time to get ready for the ball. And she felt that she also needed a break. It was hard work getting up every morning to bake batch after batch of pastries—a little taste of what running a storefront would be like. *Maybe I'll stick to catering for a while.*

Jim appeared at the window, a plastic garment bag over his shoulder. "Hey, Sofia, I wanted you to know I picked up my kilt and jacket for the ball."

Annie's face lit up. "Och, you're going to the Highland Ball, are ye? I'll see ye there, then."

"Yes, we are." Sofia leaned out to peer at the red and black plaid kilt visible through the clear covering. "I can't wait to see you in a kilt." She grinned.

He shifted uncomfortably. "It'll be the first and last time I ever wear a skirt, I can promise you that."

Annie shot Sofia a mischievous look. "Ye never know. Ye might enjoy it."

"Yeah, maybe." Jim's expression was doubtful. "Anyway, good luck with the contest. Are you coming back to the cabin after?"

Sofia had decided to let the entire family have a break by insisting she didn't need them there for the local judging portion of the contest. "Absolutely. An afternoon lounging by the water is exactly what I need."

"Marla said to tell you she'll have your easel set up." He blew her a kiss. "Good luck. Keep me posted."

"What a nice man," Annie said after Jim strode away. "Reminds me of my late husband, George, God rest his soul." With a shake of her head, she opened the oven and popped a pan of shortbread cookies inside.

Next to appear at the window was Donna with her ever-present clipboard. Sandy Wallace was with her. "Are you all set, Sofia? The judges will be around in an hour."

"Yes, I am. Oh, by the way, Annie's entry will be served here." Sofia moved over slightly so Annie could join her at the window.

Sandy frowned. "I thought you were disqualified."

"No," Annie said. "My *truck* was disqualified. Unfairly, I might add. But I wasn't, so I'm baking my cookies here. And I used all fresh ingredients from the grocery," she added quickly to forestall any criticism.

"You are each making your own shortbread, correct?" Donna asked.

"Of course," Sofia said. "I'm not letting her anywhere near my recipe." She looked at Annie, and they both laughed.

Annie patted her chest. "And I keep mine close to my vest. Literally."

Donna made a note on her clipboard. "Great. We'll see you in an hour or so."

With a final glare, Sandy followed Donna as she walked away.

Annie cackled. "Did you see the look on Sandy's face? She about died when I popped up beside you."

Was Sandy behind the mysterious mouse episodes? Would someone really be that desperate to win?

"How'd it go?" Marla asked, putting down her magazine when Sofia joined her on the front lawn. The boys were fishing along the shore, and the girls had gone into Creighton with friends to shop and sightsee.

Sofia plopped into an Adirondack chair with a sigh. "Good, I think. The judges didn't say much. There were about six of them, local dignitaries and such." She glanced at her phone. "They're supposed to call with the results."

Marla held up crossed fingers. "I'm rooting for you. Do you

feel like painting?" She gestured toward the two easels set up on the dock.

Sofia considered. It felt awfully good to sit still for a few minutes, but painting always centered her. And she could use some of that. "All right. Let's do it."

Fully absorbed in creating a watercolor of the pond, she was startled when her phone rang, displaying an unfamiliar number. Without bothering to wipe her hands, she grabbed it.

"This is Donna Roberts. I'm calling for Sofia Parker."

"Speaking." Swooping excitement hit her belly. Marla glanced over, and Sofia gave her a thumbs-up to let her know it was about the contest.

"I'm happy to tell you that you are a finalist and will be participating in the bake-off tomorrow afternoon."

Sofia sank to the dock boards, her hands shaking so much she could barely hold the phone. She had made it to the finals. She listened while Donna explained the details of the last competition.

"And who is the other finalist?" she asked after regaining her composure. With all her heart, she hoped it was her new friend, Annie.

"Sandy Wallace."

Sofia disconnected and set the phone down a safe distance from the edge of the dock. "Darn it."

"You didn't make the finals?" Marla frowned.

"I did. But Annie didn't." She felt bad for the woman. She was a good baker and nice to boot.

"Oh, Sofia." Marla shook her head. "That's too bad. But the good news is, you're in the bake-off!"

"That's right, I am." As the news sank in, a huge grin broke out over her face.

Brian came across the lawn, accompanied by the two dogs. "Hi, ladies. What's up?"

"I'm a finalist in the shortbread contest," Sofia said.

"That's fantastic. You deserve it." He rubbed his belly. "Your cookies were the best, in my opinion." He released the leashes, telling the dogs to stay, then stepped onto the dock. The dogs obeyed, lying on the grass, panting. Brian glanced at their paintings. "Wow, you're both pretty good."

"Thanks." Sofia squeezed a bit more ultramarine blue onto the palette. "Jim's gone out in the boat with the boys. They should be back soon."

"I'll hang out here for a while, if that's okay." He sat, removing his sneakers and dangling his feet in the clear water. "Ah. That feels good." He stared across at dark clouds over the hills across the pond. "Looks like a thunderstorm building."

"Cloud castles, I called them when I was a little girl," Marla said. She swirled a little black into her white paint.

"Are you going to the ball tonight, Brian?" Sofia asked. "We'll all be there."

"I'm going with Wendell." Marla's laugh was a joyful tinkle. "Do you know him?"

Sofia winced. She still hadn't told Marla about Brian's history with Madelaine and his resentment of Wendell.

"Of course I'll be there." Brian's tone was glum and his shoulders sagged. "It won't be the same this year, though."

"You mean without Madelaine?" Sofia raised her brows at Marla, who nodded to indicate she now understood.

"Yep. That's exactly what I mean." He splashed his feet back and forth. "I have something to get off my chest, if you're willing to listen, Sofia."

Sofia pulse sped up. What did he know about Madelaine's death? Had he been there? "Of course, Brian. We're family."

He expelled a huge sigh. "Can someone have a heart attack if you yell at them?"

"If that was true, Jim would've had one a long time ago." Sofia attempted a laugh.

"I never told anybody this," he said slowly. "But I saw Madelaine that day. I was at the fairgrounds and happened to see her going into the food truck. She was all friendly and 'How are you?' as if nothing ever happened between us. Then she told me she was going to marry Wendell."

Marla gasped, then covered it with a cough. Sofia felt a sharp pang of sadness too at hearing that Wendell and Madelaine had been headed toward happily ever after.

"That must have been hard." Sofia put down her palette and sat beside him on the dock. Reaching out, she took his hand.

Brian ducked his head, and she thought she saw the shimmer of tears. "It was. But it doesn't excuse what I did."

The silence stretched out uncomfortably until Sofia finally spoke. "What happened?"

"I screamed at her. I called her every name in the book. I even called her a homewrecker, which to her was even worse than the rest because I knew she felt guilty about hurting Sandy Wallace."

"Perhaps she should have felt guilty," Sofia countered. "She did break up a marriage, after all."

Brian snorted. "Not really. Wendell and Sandy were separated. In fact, he lived in New York state for over a year. Then he moved his business back . . . and, well, you know the rest." He sighed again. "Thanks for listening. I've been feeling horrible ever since it happened, like I caused her death."

"I don't think it was your fault, Brian." Down the shoreline, Sofia heard the hum of a small fishing boat approaching. *Probably Jim and the boys on their way back.* She remembered what Wendell said about Madelaine's illness. "How did she seem otherwise? Someone else told me she was coming down with the flu that weekend." She didn't mention it was his rival.

"She seemed okay. A little draggy, come to think of it." He stared at the pond through squinted eyes. "She did say something weird. She said her eyes were acting up. Everything looked yellow."

"Yellow vision? That sounds like poison to me." Marla picked up her phone. "Let me call the library. I'll have my assistant look it up."

Julie had arrived, and the three friends were relaxing on the cabin deck while Mark, Jim, and Brian hung out on the dock.

"You really think Madelaine was poisoned?" Julie's green eyes were wide. "And nobody put that together, including the doctors."

Marla strolled away and spoke quietly into her phone. "Yes, the reference book . . . that's the one."

"I suppose they took the heart attack at face value," Sofia said. "It doesn't sound like anyone who knew her well was there when it happened."

"That's true." Julie shook her head. "It takes suspicious minds like ours to think of such a thing." She glanced over as Marla strolled back to join them. "What did you find out?"

Marla's face was grim. "The yellow vision is a symptom of long-term digitalis poisoning."

"Digitalis? Isn't that heart medicine?" Sofia remembered a friend of her grandmother's taking it.

"It is." Marla sat in her folding chair and propped her bare feet on the deck railing. "One of the medicines derived from botanicals. Foxglove."

"I grow foxglove." Sofia thought of tall spikes characterized by yellow or pink tubular blossoms, a common sight in Vermont summer gardens. Then shock froze her core. Had someone doctored the herbal supplements she'd found? "You won't believe this, but if we're right, the murder weapon is in my food truck."

"Did you get the goods?" Julie asked when Sofia and Jim joined the Butlers at their table. The dinner and ball were being held at the elegant, historic Creighton Inn.

"Sure did. The pill bottle is safely locked in the glove compartment." Sofia glanced around the spacious dining room, which was thronged with men in Highland evening wear and women in semiformal dress. She saw Brian, Laura, and Sandy as well as other faces she recognized from the games. "Is Marla here yet?" Wendell had picked her up at the cabin.

"Here they come," Julie said as the couple appeared in the doorway.

Wendell was in full regalia, including his bagpipe. As he crossed the room, he received many glances of appreciation. After escorting Marla to her chair, he greeted the others. "I'll be back after I perform the opening piece." He slipped back outside.

"I feel like I'm in a movie," Marla confided as Wendell strode away.

"Like *Braveheart*?" Julie quipped.

"I feel like I need to cover my legs," Jim said, tugging on the hem of his kilt. "How do you women stand it?"

Sofia laughed. "Cut it out. You look gorgeous." She took in Jim's outfit—the lace jabot, fitted black jacket, and red and black MacGregor tartan kilt.

"I agree," Julie said before turning to her husband, Mark.

"And so do you." The contrast between his blond hair and black jacket was flattering.

He smiled at her compliment and flipped at the jabot. "Never thought I'd be caught wearing lace. But hey, I'll try anything once."

"I disagree," Sofia said. "I think we should make wearing Highland regalia a regular thing." She laughed at Jim's appalled face, then hushed as a lone bagpipe keened *The Flower of Scotland*. As Wendell made his grand entrance into the dining room, everyone rose. The celebration was under way.

After a fabulous dinner of grilled trout, seared rare beef, and assorted vegetables, the group adjourned to the ballroom. Since a small symphony was playing most of the music, Wendell was free to dance. And dance they did—reels and circle dances and waltzes.

"Now this is definitely something I'd like to do again soon," Sofia said as Jim whirled her around in his arms. Their friends danced nearby, and to all appearances, they were having a great time also.

"It is fun." Jim huffed and puffed a little as they stepped down off the dance floor. "Great exercise too." His kilt swayed with his movements, revealing handsome knees.

She rolled her eyes. "You're so romantic."

Jim pulled her close and gave her a warm kiss. "How's that for romantic?"

"Very nice, Laird Parker." They smiled at each other, and Sofia felt a surge of happy contentment. *What a wonderful husband.*

Then she heard a woman cry for help, cries that escalated until they could be heard over the music, which ground to a discordant halt.

Was that . . . Marla?

Sofia and Jim ran into the fray. Along with the other dancers, they crowded close to an unsettling sight.

Wendell lay face up on the floor, eyes closed. Was he unconscious . . . or dead?

18

Edinburgh, Scotland
September 1745

The prince's secretary gave no sign that he recognized Isabelle. "Have a seat and wait. He's with someone right now."

Isabelle waved the letter at him. "But he summoned me and said it was urgent."

Mr. Murray glanced at the letter and handed it back, his lips twisting in derision. "That was before Dr. Donaldson decided he needed an immediate audience."

Dr. Donaldson! Was he reporting his conversation with William to the prince? That seemed rash, if he did indeed care about William and his mother.

A terrible temptation thrust its way into Isabelle's mind. If the doctor was here . . .

"I'll be back shortly. I, uh, need . . ." She let her words drift off, knowing that the man wouldn't care to inquire too deeply into the cause of her exit.

"Down the hall and to the left." He bent over his work, his nib scratching across the paper.

Isabelle didn't go down the hall and to the left. Instead, she went to the right and climbed the stairs to the secondary rooms on the next floor. She didn't allow herself to think too deeply about her rash actions. She merely put one foot in front of the other with a silent prayer that she would get away with her plan.

The upper hallway was dark, no lamps lit yet against the encroaching darkness. Most people were out and about on their business still, but she knew she didn't have long. Any minute now, they would return to the castle to wash and dress for the night's festivities. She didn't even see Bess, who must have been toiling in the kitchen at this hour, peeling potatoes or turning a roast on a spit.

Dr. Donaldson's chambers were at the end of the hallway, she knew. With any luck, he hadn't locked the door since he was in residence. *Aha.* The door to the outer chamber swung open easily with one twist of the knob.

Before entering, she glanced behind her, then peered down the long corridor, ears straining for any sign of his return. It wouldn't do at all to be caught here. She had no excuse to invade his private chambers.

Only a suspicion of murder.

The outer room was where the doctor met patients. It held his desk, a few cabinets, and a screen, beyond which was the high, hard bed used for examinations. The tin of salve used by the White Hart's landlord should be in one of the cabinets, if he'd saved it. She was relying on the doctor to regard it as too costly to throw away. It might well be given to another patient.

The cabinets held medicines, as she suspected, but they were all in a jumble, not in alphabetical order as was her preference. Bottles, tins, jars, and boxes were crammed in without regard to application or purpose. *How on earth does he find anything?* Maybe they'd been piled in here when he moved in and he hadn't straightened them out yet.

Shivering with nerves, she pawed through the medications as quickly as possible. Resisting the urge to skip around, she forced herself to begin on the left and work methodically to the right. Her salve tin was small and slender and might easily have been hidden by larger objects or even slipped down behind a shelf.

The doorknob rattled. *Oh, why didn't I lock it?* She glanced around, seeking escape. Behind the screen? But what if he had a patient with him?

The bedchamber. The urge to run flashed over her in a white-hot rush of fear that lent wings to her feet. She dashed into the room and rolled herself under the bed, thankful it was quite high off the floor. The heavy satin bedspread hung to the floor, so he wouldn't spot her underneath. She pushed aside the folds to see out.

The bedroom door was ajar, giving her a good view of Donaldson entering the outer room. His gaze immediately went to the jumble of boxes and bandages on the carpet. She must have knocked them out of the cabinet in her haste to escape.

He glanced around the room, then bent with a groan to pick up the items one by one, and shoved them back onto the shelf with no regard to order. "Useless maids," he muttered. After he finished, he slammed the cabinet door and rose with a grunt. One hand pressed to his lower back, he tottered out of her line of vision. Hearing the creak of the chair, she assumed he was sitting at his desk.

Now what? He might sit out there for hours, writing or whatever it was he did to pass the time. The prince must be wondering where she had gone, a thought that added urgency to her plight. Otherwise she might as well take a nap in her dark and comfortable nest until the doctor left for dinner. He had to eat sometime, that much was certain.

But since the prince was waiting, she needed to get out of there. Obviously she couldn't go out the way she'd entered, so she needed another exit. Scooting backward, she peered out the left side of the bed. In that direction, she saw two windows with a wardrobe standing between them. They were three floors up, so going out the window wouldn't work. She'd never survive the fall.

She moved to the right and pushed aside the spread. Her heart lifted in hope when she caught sight of a door next to the fireplace. *That must lead somewhere, either to a dressing room or an adjoining bedroom.* She hoped from there, she could get back out to the hallway.

She stared at the door for what seemed an eternity, trying to gather enough courage to leave her snug hiding place. Donaldson couldn't see her from where he was sitting, but he might hear her. What if the floor creaked or the door squeaked? *Can I sneak without a creak or squeak?* She bit back a gasp of hysterical laughter at her foolish rhyme.

It was time to leave before she lost her wits from the strain and gave herself away. Lying on her stomach, she pushed herself out from under the bed using both hands and feet. Then she crawled to the door, sliding her hands and knees along rather than lifting them up and down.

Rising onto her knees, she twisted the knob oh so slowly, ready to release it at the slightest sound and scramble back under the bed. When the metal turned silently, she mentally praised the consideration of those who lubricated the castle hardware. It was a miracle, really, considering the state of almost everything else at Holyrood.

She pushed the door open, again wincing in anticipation of a noise that would reveal her presence. Fortunately, the hinges swung inward with equal ease, revealing a darkened room. She threw herself through the doorway. When the door clicked shut behind her, she collapsed onto her back with a gasp, her heart thumping in gratitude that her gamble had succeeded.

A light flared, causing Isabelle to shriek in surprise.

"I will refrain from asking why you are lying on the floor," a deep voice said. "But I must say it is an odd method of paying a call."

Isabelle turned her head to see Rory MacGregor looming over her, a candlestick in his hand. She sat bolt upright, flaming with mortification. "What are you doing here?"

One brow lifted. "That is my question, milady, since you are in my chamber."

A hot flush traveled up Isabelle's chest and into her cheeks. "In your chamber? Oh my. I had no idea where that door led, I assure you."

Someone banged on the door. "MacGregor! Is everything all right in there?"

Oh no. Donaldson had heard her yell. And after she'd managed to be so quiet.

Isabelle scrambled to her feet, gazing around frantically. "What should I do? Where should I go?"

"I take it you prefer not to see the good doctor?"

"In here? Of course not." Besides the fact that she had been in the doctor's bedchamber without invitation, it would do her reputation no good to be caught in Rory's. "Please, help me."

His grin was annoyingly smug. "On one condition. You tell me exactly what is going on."

She flapped her hands at him impatiently, shifting from foot to foot in anxiety. "I will, I promise."

"Hide behind the curtains." He pointed to the floor-length velvet drapes, and she scurried to comply, concealing herself as he opened the door. Try as she might, she could see nothing through the fabric's thick, dense weave. She hoped the same was true from the opposite side so Donaldson wouldn't spot her. She thrust her heels back tight against the wall so her toes wouldn't peep out.

"What on earth is going on over here? I thought I heard a woman scream." Donaldson sounded annoyed.

Rory laughed. "The maid was dropping off fresh linens, and I startled her."

"Well, tell her to bring me some if you see her again. Right now I have to get back to work." A pause. "Did you see anyone going into my chamber?"

"No, I didn't spot anyone . . . going in." That devil. She knew he said it like that for her benefit. "Why do you ask?"

"Someone has been going through my medicine cabinet. I found things scattered all over the floor."

"You should keep your door locked, doctor. You never know whom you might find prowling around the castle." His voice held a definite note of amusement, again to tweak her, Isabelle was certain.

"Thank you for your sage advice. Good day." The door banged shut.

"You can come out now."

Isabelle gratefully pulled the curtains aside and stepped into the much cooler air of the room. "I can explain."

Rory crossed his arms. "Please do."

She filled him in on how she'd taken advantage of the doctor's absence to search for the tin of salve among his medicines. "I was trying to see if we could clear him."

"Or implicate him." Rory gave her that infuriating grin again. "Why are you here to see the prince?"

She had hoped to gloss over that point, but he was too smart by half. She dropped her gaze, unable to look him in the eye. "I cannot say. It is a confidential matter."

In one stride, he crossed the room to stand in front of her. He tipped her chin up with one finger. "Has our handsome monarch turned your pretty head, my dear?"

Is that what he thinks? How ridiculous. Her laugh was brittle as she pulled away. "Of course not. It is a matter of state security." The awareness that she'd told her cousin all about it sat like a stone in her belly, but she didn't dare confide in Rory. He might feel obliged to inform the prince of her indiscretion. It wasn't fair to William to share the prince's doubts about his loyalty either.

Rory didn't say anything for a long moment. With every passing second, Isabelle's wretchedness grew. During the past few days, she had sensed something tender blossoming between them, too small and delicate to be called love, perhaps, but special all the same. The very real possibility that her secret might kill their growing relationship stabbed like a dagger between her ribs.

She moved toward the door. "I must go. It does not do to keep a king waiting, does it?" Again she heard the brittle tenor in her laughter. "I will see you tonight?" She held her breath, waiting for his reply. What if he decided he didn't want anything more to do with her? With a sudden rush of remorse, she ran to him and grasped both of his hands in hers. "If I could tell you, I would. Please, trust me."

His warm fingers tightened on hers. "I believe you, my dear. And yes, I will see you at dinner tonight."

"Would anyone like a glass of sherry?" Isabelle asked her guests. She stood at the sideboard in the parlor where they were relaxing in front of the fire before dinner. Margaret and Harry sat close together on a sofa while Rory was in one of the fireside wing chairs.

"I would," Margaret said. Harry and Rory assented.

"How are you feeling after your ordeal earlier today?" Harry asked as Isabelle approached with a silver tray holding four half-filled glasses.

Which one? She knew he meant the runaway horse. "I am a little sore, but I should be fine by tomorrow." She handed the couple their drinks.

"Thank goodness you were there," Margaret said to Rory. She shuddered. "Isabelle might have broken her neck."

Rory smiled a thank-you as Isabelle served him. "Glad I could be of service." He winked, and she knew he was also referring to her narrow escape from Donaldson's chamber. Would she ever live that fiasco down? By the amusement on his face, she guessed not.

"The new Lord Lochmere was useless," Margaret said as Isabelle took her own seat, the matching wing chair across from Rory. "He didn't even discern that something was wrong with the horse." She set her untouched sherry on the end table with a clatter. "Are his political views as muddled, Isabelle? What does the prince think?"

So much for being discreet. Isabelle felt her face heat up at Rory's astonished stare. She refused to meet his eyes. "Thanks for letting the cat out of the bag, cousin."

Margaret clapped a hand over her mouth. "I am so sorry."

Harry quickly caught on. "William hasn't taken the oath of allegiance yet, has he? And I'm guessing you were deputized to find out where he stood, Isabelle."

Isabelle set down her own drink and quickly crossed the room to close the parlor door. "What I say must not leave this room. Are you in agreement, Margaret?"

Margaret squirmed in her seat. "Of course. I said I was sorry. Besides, we can trust Harry and Rory." She touched Harry on the arm. "Can't we?"

Harry put his hand on his chest. "I swear it on my mother's life. Not a word of it shall pass these lips."

Rory snorted at the couple's histrionics. "I am surprised to learn our sovereign is recruiting women as spies. That said, I must agree that Isabelle is a remarkably astute choice."

"Thanks, I think." Isabelle crossed to her chair and sat. "I'm not sure how much thought he put into it. I went to him out of concern about Lochmere's death, and he enlisted me. What could I say?"

Harry didn't know about the salve, so Isabelle filled him in on the investigation. They all hashed over the fact that no one except Ogilvy had been cleared. Then the discussion returned to William.

"I was shocked when he bluntly told Donaldson that he hadn't made up his mind," Isabelle said. "I was rather afraid to tell the prince, but I made sure I quoted him exactly as I remembered. He can decide what to make of it."

"In all justice to William, it is a momentous decision to join the Jacobites," Harry said, his lively face suddenly somber. "We are putting everything we hold dear on the line in this fight."

"I can't bear to think about the possibility of losing," Rory said. "And I must confess I sometimes think we are all plunging over a cliff with our eyes shut."

His honesty struck a chord of fear in Isabelle. If they did lose, what kinds of reprisals would the English enact? For a mad moment, she wished they could send the prince back to France and pretend nothing had happened. Then she composed herself. Her mother would roll over in her grave if she could hear her daughter's disloyal and cowardly thoughts.

"We must fight, or submit to English domination for another hundred years or more." Harry's fist clenched on his knee as he stared into the fire. "What they have done to countless families—my own included—is unconscionable."

They all fell silent, lost in thought. Then Isabelle roused herself. This would not do; she owed her guests a pleasant evening. She rose to her feet. "Enough of politics and war. Tonight we are alive and well and together. What more do we need?"

The maid chose that fortuitous moment to knock and announce dinner. "We have two more guests, milady. Your father has brought Mr. McTavish home with him to dine."

"That's wonderful." Archibald McTavish was a historian and bard and an old family friend. Still, everyone, no matter how close the friendship, called him Mr. McTavish. Isabelle adored him.

Perhaps it was the anticipation of a good meal, but the others threw off their melancholy and chatted merrily as they made their way to the dining room. Isabelle's heart lifted at the sight of the welcoming room. At her direction, the maid had used the best linen, silver, china, and crystal to set the table. A roaring fire and candles provided enough light to be flattering while allowing the diners to actually see their food.

"This is lovely," Margaret said.

Everyone took their seats while introductions were made. Small talk passed easily over the soup course of Scotch broth.

"An excellent choice, my dear, especially on a night as cold as this," Mr. McTavish said, gray eyes twinkling behind his spectacles. He wore his white, wispy hair swept over his brow. As usual, his cravat was tied right up to his chin. Mr. McTavish had a horror of drafts and taking cold.

"I'm glad you could join us," Isabelle said. "You too, Papa. He's been out playing engagements almost every night," she told the others.

"You have a fine orchestra," Rory said. "It rivals those I have heard on the continent in Paris and Rome."

Isabelle wasn't aware Rory had traveled to Europe. What else didn't she know about the man? She relished the thought of getting to know him better. *Perhaps once all these travails are behind us . . .*

Sebastian Ripa inclined his head. "Thank you. I am from Italy, so perhaps I brought some of that savoir faire with me."

The maid cleared the bowls and brought in the main course consisting of a large, fine beef roast, Yorkshire pudding, gravy, and boiled carrots and potatoes. At Isabelle's request, she left the platters and bowls in the middle of the table to be passed around, rather than serve them.

"What a wonderful feast." Harry heaped his plate with several thick slices of beef. Then he paused, the serving fork thrust into a particularly golden and puffy piece of pudding. "If we're all patriots here, shouldn't this dish be called Edinburghshire pudding?" He referred to the fact that Yorkshire was an English county.

Everyone laughed. "Pass me some of that Edinburghshire pudding, lad," Mr. McTavish said.

"How have you been, Mr. McTavish?" Isabelle asked as they all tucked in. "I haven't seen you for ages."

"I am doing quite well, my dear. I was at my country house most of the summer, working on another book." He paused. "A history of the Stuarts."

"What fortuitous timing," Rory said. "Did you have advance notice of the prince's arrival?" He smiled to show he was joking.

"Oh no, certainly not. But current events might well boost its circulation, which makes my publisher happy. Rising tide and all that."

"Mr. McTavish has some interesting information to share, Isabelle." Sebastian gave his daughter a significant look from his end of the table. "It's about the history of the Lochmere family."

Isabelle felt a rush of excitement. Perhaps their friend could provide further clues to Lochmere's untimely demise.

Mr. McTavish pushed his spectacles up on his nose. "Let me say this: If I were to write a book about the late Lord Lochmere, it would be titled *Justice Served*."

Harry, not familiar with the historian's brusque manner, objected. "I say, isn't that rather harsh? The man is dead, after all."

"And so we all shall be, sooner or later." Mr. McTavish's glare was repressive. "What is history but the stories of departed men and women?"

Sebastian waved his fork and knife. "Eat up and listen. I promise it will be worth your time."

Mr. McTavish gave a summary of the dead man's early years and detailed some of the stories Isabelle had heard at the sewing circle about his cruelty to tenants and his remorseless revenge against enemies.

"He was a royal beast, for certain." Harry's eyes were wide.

"I'm surprised there wasn't a mob chasing him to France with flaming torches and pitchforks," Rory added.

"I would have been in the front of the crowd, if so," Isabelle said. Although she had heard the stories once already, they outraged her again.

"As would I," Margaret said. She mimed the thrust of a pitchfork, hissing.

"Such men often evade punishment. It's one of the mysteries of the world." Mr. McTavish paused. "But I have not told you the worst tale."

Isabelle's heart skipped a beat. Was it about Lochmere's wife? She'd meant to ask Grannie to expand upon the tale, but she hadn't seen the woman since the sewing circle.

All eyes were upon him as he continued. "He married a widow with the misfortune to own much property in her own right."

Isabelle caught her breath. Yes, it was the same story. What was so horrible that Grannie wouldn't tell it?

"When she didn't prove as compliant or as helpful as he wished regarding acceptance by her clan," Mr. McTavish continued, "he had her judged insane and locked her in a tower to starve, which she did in short order."

Isabelle and Margaret gasped, and the men swore softly under their breath.

"Of course, the official cause of death was listed as derangement. Otherwise, Lochmere would have gone to the gallows." He thumped the table with his fist. "I have the word of a trusted source regarding this matter. The doctor who attended her."

They all broke into excited chatter.

Sebastian held up his hand. "You haven't heard the rest. Go on, Mr. McTavish."

"The woman had a young daughter. She is now known as Lady Fiona Ross."

19

Edinburgh, Scotland
September 1745

With Mr. McTavish's last words, everything fell into place in Isabelle's mind. His story gave Lady Fiona a compelling motive for killing Lord Lochmere. How she must have hated him for causing her mother's death and fleeing the country beyond the reach of justice! Had she planned to kill him all along, or was the salve a temptation too great to resist?

Then Isabelle remembered a piece of information that made her blood run cold.

She shoved back her chair and stood. "Please excuse me, everyone. I need to check something." Without waiting to see their reaction, she threw down her napkin and fled the room, followed by exclamations of surprise.

She dashed down the hallway and up the stairs to her workroom, ignoring the pinch of her corset against her ribs. She threw open the door and dashed to the shelf for her ledger, pulled it down, and leafed through the pages to the date of Lady Fiona's purchase.

Her breath caught. As she feared, Lady Fiona had ordered another medicine that could be poisonous if misused.

Tansy tea, prescribed for Lady Fiona's female complaint.

With her focus on the salve, she hadn't paid attention to the rest of the order. *What a foolish oversight!* If her terrible suspicion about Lady Fiona's intention was correct, there was no time to lose. Even now it might be too late.

With a desperate prayer that she would be in time, she grabbed mustard powder and salt and threw them into a basket. An effective and safe remedy, if administered soon enough.

Despite her earlier decision to not ride a horse for a good long while, within fifteen minutes, Isabelle and Rory, who had joined her as she fled her home, were riding across town toward Lady Fiona's house on Castle Terrace behind Edinburgh Castle. Margaret and Harry had wanted to come, but Isabelle thought a large entourage would alert the noblewoman to their true motives. Her pretext was a message from her father inviting Lady Fiona to dine. Unless needed, Rory would wait outside.

"You really think she might try to hurt William?" Rory asked as they slowed the horses to a walk.

Isabelle scanned both sides of the street for the right number. "Yes, I do. After I heard Mr. McTavish's story, I believe she killed Lord Lochmere in revenge. But even if not, you would think she would shun his brother. But she is doing exactly the opposite, flirting with him and asking him to dine."

"I wonder if I should be worried then." His tone was deadpan.

Isabelle let out a bark of surprised laughter. "Well said." She reined in her mare in front of the house, which was dark except for a flickering light in the back. She dismounted and tied her horse to a post.

"Do you think she's home?" Rory slid off his horse and joined her at the door.

"We'll soon find out." Isabelle banged the door knocker several times.

A burly male servant answered, giving an odd flinch when he saw Isabelle. Then she recognized him—Lady Fiona had sent him to collect her order.

"Lady Fiona is not receiving visitors," he said.

Isabelle waved the letter at him. "I have a message for her from my father."

"I will take it to her." He reached for it but Isabelle snatched it out of reach.

"I was instructed to deliver it into her hands." Isabelle stepped through the doorway, forcing her way past the man. He tried to block her passage, but at a growl from Rory, he dropped back.

Isabelle trotted along the dark hallway, heading for the glow of light in the rear where Lady Fiona must be, probably in a parlor or sitting room. The thud of footsteps behind her let her know that Rory had decided to follow.

Gruesome visions of what she might find flashed through her head, causing her steps to falter. William, dead on the carpet or writhing in agony from poison. Or maybe she had imagined the whole thing and the couple was chatting quietly by the fireside or, embarrassing for all concerned, locked in a romantic clinch.

Then she thought about Lord Lochmere, dead before his time, and the missing salve. She must complete her mission regardless of any social humiliation or upset.

The room's door was half open, and Isabelle burst through without knocking, another social faux pas for certain.

Lady Fiona Ross lounged in an upholstered chair, staring into a dying fire. A trio of candles flickered on a nearby table. She was alone.

Isabelle noticed the setting for an informal dinner for two on a low table with part of a loaf of bread and some roasted chicken remaining. Someone else had dined with her; that much was obvious.

"Where is William?"

Lady Fiona turned her head, barely seeming to absorb Isabelle's presence. What was wrong with her? "He is gone," she said at last, her tone flat and emotionless.

Fear jolted Isabelle. "What do you mean? Is he dead?"

The other woman pushed herself to a more upright position, her face puzzled. "No, he left." Her gaze traveled over Isabelle's shoulder and she nodded. "Lord MacGregor."

Isabelle felt like sinking through the carpet. She had made a total fool of herself barging in like this, not even remembering to mention the excuse of her father's message.

Lady Fiona seemed to have regained her wits. "Why do you ask if he is dead? How odd."

"His brother did recently die under strange circumstances, Lady Fiona," Rory said. "We were worried that William might fall victim to the same fate."

Spots of color appeared on Lady Fiona's cheeks. "I thought Lochmere died of heart failure. What makes you think it was something else?"

Without invitation, Isabelle sat in the fireside chair that William probably has occupied earlier since the place setting was in front of it. "We have reason to believe that he was poisoned. Dr. Donaldson agrees," she lied.

"They are exhuming the body for an examination," Rory said, moving farther into the room. "The prince will sign the order tomorrow."

Lady Fiona shuddered. "How ghastly." In the firelight, Isabelle thought she saw a flash of fear in Lady Fiona's green eyes.

Firelight glistened on the half-full teacup left in William's place. On an impulse, she picked it up and sniffed it. She was struck by the strong odor of tansy. She'd know it anywhere.

Isabelle jumped to her feet. "This tea is toxic. We must find William immediately." A choking sob rose in her chest. "Before it is too late." The only saving grace was that tansy would take hours to poison someone.

Lady Fiona launched herself from her chair. "Toxic? What on earth do you mean?"

"Rory, you are my witness. William drank tansy tea."

Suddenly, Lady Fiona grabbed the carving knife and stabbed with it toward Isabelle and Rory. "You are not going anywhere." With her other hand, she reached for the bell pull and jerked on it.

The servant bolted into the room. His cry of "Milady!" was cut short by Rory's shoulder block. The men began to grapple with grunts and shouts. Lady Fiona advanced on Isabelle, the long, sharp blade flashing in the candlelight. It was up to Isabelle to subdue her, since Rory and the other man were evenly matched.

Isabelle scanned the room for a weapon. A teapot, plates, and a half-eaten chicken were no match for that knife. She picked up the teapot anyway and heaved it at the other woman, who ducked. The porcelain pot fell to the rug, splashing its contents everywhere. Lady Fiona stepped closer, pushing Isabelle back toward the fireplace. The heat penetrated her dress, almost burning her legs.

The fire. She glanced down to the set of fireplace tools. Could she do it?

Lady Fiona thrust the knife forward, slicing into Isabelle's bodice.

She had no choice.

With a deft, lightning-fast movement, she picked up the shovel, scooped several glowing coals, and threw them at Lady Fiona. The woman shrieked and fell back, dropping the knife as she brushed frantically at her skirts. One stubborn coal lingered, igniting the silky fabric. Lady Fiona shrieked again, and the distraction enabled Rory to gain the upper hand with the servant.

Isabelle didn't want the woman to burn to death, so she kicked the knife away and tugged down the curtains, then launched herself at Lady Fiona. She brought her to the ground using the heavy velvet to smother the flames.

Lady Fiona lay on the carpet, moaning and writhing. Rory

secured the servant's hands with his belt, then helped Isabelle tear away the charred fabric.

"Not as bad as I feared," Isabelle said after examining the woman's lower legs. "The skin will blister, but it will heal." She patted Lady Fiona's shoulder. "I will send over some burn salve."

"And the constable," Rory said.

Lady Fiona reared up with a snarl. "You're mad!" She lurched toward Isabelle, and Rory was forced to restrain her. "I have done nothing!"

Isabelle dodged away, heading for the door. "Oh yes, you did. But I don't have time to argue. I need to find William right away if I am to save his life."

"He is lodging in his brother's chamber at Holyrood," Rory said. At Isabelle's start of surprise, he added, "The prince wanted to keep him under observation. You go take care of him. I will stand guard here and wait for the watch."

At the mention of the watch, Lady Fiona snarled again but subsided upon Rory's glare.

"I will send them right away," Isabelle promised. She dashed down the hallway and out to her horse. She was climbing into the saddle when she heard two riders clattering down the street on horseback. As they passed under a streetlamp, she recognized Harry and Margaret.

"I know you said not to come, but we got worried," Margaret called.

"I am glad you did." She quickly filled them in.

Margaret was horrified. "That wildcat might have killed you, Isabelle."

"I know. I guess our plan wasn't very sensible after all. However, I need to hurry to William." She was fairly twitching with eagerness to give him the antidote to the tansy. There was no telling how much he had ingested.

"What do you want me to do?" Harry asked.

"Help Rory keep Lady Fiona and her servant under control. Margaret, come with me. On the way to the palace, we will look for the watch and send them over to arrest Lady Fiona." She and Margaret wheeled their horses around and set off at a brisk trot. The watch patrolled the streets at night, and it wasn't long before they came across a pair of men near the head of the Royal Mile.

Isabelle told them the address, saying it was a case of murder and that she and Lady Margaret were continuing on to the palace to conduct the prince's business. The two watchmen set off at a run, shouting the alarm for others to join them. Then Isabelle and Margaret pounded down the road to Holyrood.

"Is Lord Lochmere in residence?" Isabelle asked the guard at the main door. "We need to see him immediately. It is a matter of life and death."

"I am not sure, milady." The man looked dubious about letting two women into the castle so late at night. "This is a wee bit irregular."

Isabelle stamped her foot impatiently. "Lord MacGregor sent me." She thrust her basket toward him. "I am here on a medical mission. We believe Lord William has been poisoned."

"What is that you say? Poisoned?" In the flickering torchlight, his mouth turned down in disbelief. "That is news to me."

She decided to try persuasion since the bald truth was obviously not succeeding. Moving closer, she lowered her voice to a confiding, wheedling tone. "I know you are simply doing your job, and you are doing it well. Why not ask the prince if we can come in?" She gestured to the brightly lit windows above. "Obviously he has not yet retired for the evening."

He gave that some thought but didn't budge from his wide-legged stance.

"You are being daft, my good man," Margaret blurted. "His

Majesty will be angry if you do not let her pass. She is doing special work on his behalf."

"All right. But if you are lying . . ." He went inside, making sure to close the door firmly so they couldn't sneak in.

"I am not lying!" Isabelle yelled. "And by all the saints, you had best let me in!" She kicked the door a few times for good measure, then banged it with her fist. Then she screamed at the top of her lungs, not caring if she sounded like a raging fishwife. She screamed so long and loud that her throat ached.

Margaret stared at her in amazement. "My goodness, Isabelle. I have never seen you lose your temper."

"You would lose your temper too." A despairing sob rattled her chest, escaping in a hiccup. Ever since Lochmere's death and the realization that her medicine had been used to murder a man, she'd been soldiering along under a staggering heap of fear, dismay, and guilt. Now she had reached the breaking point. Another man was about to die, and she was helpless to stop it.

A window slid up above their heads. "What is all that ruckus down there?"

"Prince Charles?" Margaret's face was rapturous. "Please let us in."

When Bonnie Prince Charlie, followed by Isabelle and Margaret, burst into William's chamber, they found him writhing on the bed, clutching his belly, his face slick with sweat. His cheeks were bright red, another sign of tansy poisoning. He didn't comment on their sudden appearance, and Isabelle noticed to her dismay that his eyes displayed the distant, dilated glare of someone nearing death. They had arrived barely in time.

"Get me water!" she barked, pulling out the mustard and salt. As Margaret scurried to comply, she measured the dry powders into the cup she'd brought. Then she mixed the brew and with the prince's help, got most of it down William's throat. To her surprise, the prince insisted on holding the basin while William vomited; he did not seem to care if his fine shirt was splashed and soiled.

Finally William rolled back onto the pillows with a gasp. His eyes flickered open, widening when he saw who was standing at his bedside. "Lady Isabelle? Why are you here?"

She smoothed warm blankets over his shoulders. "You drank something bad, William, and we purged your stomach." To Margaret she said, "Please go fetch some coffee from the kitchen."

"'Twas Lady Fiona, was it not?" William struggled to sit up. "I thought something was wrong—"

"Lie down and rest, William," the prince said, stepping forward into the candlelight. The basin had been disposed of, and the prince looked as pristine as ever. "You have been through quite an ordeal." Judging by his kind and sympathetic expression, no one would have guessed he doubted the other man's loyalty enough to ask Isabelle to spy on him.

William's mouth dropped at the sight of the prince in his bedchamber. "Your Majesty." He reached his hand out in supplication. "I assure you . . . I will take the oath."

The prince held up his hand. "Tomorrow is soon enough to think about such matters." He turned to Isabelle. "Thank you for your service, both to your fellow man and to me. Scotland is fortunate to have women as brave and loyal as you."

London, England, June 1747

The rowdy crowd waiting outside the prison gates jostled Isabelle, forcing her to fight for her tiny square of pavement. Most of them regarded the release of pardoned Jacobites as a sport comparable to tormenting stray dogs. Others—women, children, a few men, Isabelle, and Margaret—waited in agonizing hope and impatience to see loved ones again. Loved ones who by some grace had escaped death on the battlefield, transportation to the Colonies, and execution.

Bonnie Prince Charlie's campaign for the throne had collapsed upon the bloody battlefield of Culloden on April 16, 1746, after which the Jacobites had been hunted and imprisoned. The bonnie prince himself had escaped to France disguised as a lady's maid, an ignoble end to his brave attempt to seize what he regarded as his birthright. His supporters were left behind to fend for themselves.

Margaret gripped her arm. "Do you think they will really let them out? What if it is another cruel joke?" Margaret, like everyone else, was pale and drawn, so much thinner than she had once been that her once-fashionable dress hung on her like a sack. But she was still lovely, her eyes lit by ardent love for the imprisoned Harry Campbell.

"They were on the list. So let us pray." Isabelle winced as a heavyset woman trod on her foot without apology.

Isabelle detested London with a passion, repelled by its uncouth citizens, crowded crooked streets, and sheer filth. At the same time, she knew they had been fortunate to escape Edinburgh.

Thanks to the support of her father's patrons, he was now well settled in an orchestra and, as a native-born Italian, had escaped censure. But she missed Scotland with a fierce yearning that throbbed in her blood and bone. She longed for the sight of misty lochs nestled in abrupt, heather-covered hills, to hear the wail of the pipes and the curlew's haunting cry. She'd lost both her home and her heritage.

And she'd almost lost Rory MacGregor.

The gates opened and a straggling line of prisoners began to shamble out, some limping, others supporting friends. Wearing the plaid was now illegal, so they were dressed in plain-woven rags. The English began to jeer and hoot. But the Scots among the crowd fell dead silent, eyes straining for a glimpse of a beloved face.

"There he is! There they are!" Margaret wailed, tears running down her face. Isabelle's gaze followed Margaret's pointing finger to the two men, one slightly taller than the other, one with red hair, the other dark. She picked up her skirts and ran, elbowing and shoving her way through tightly pressed bodies, Margaret at her heels.

She saw Harry nudge Rory.

When Rory's eyes fastened on hers, she saw nothing beyond his beaming smile, white against his dirty face. He held his arms open wide and she flew into them, heedless of the prison stench that clung to his clothes and body.

"Is it you, lass? Is it really you?" His face held a heartbreaking expression of adoring disbelief.

"It is." She tightened her arms around him. "And I will never leave your side again."

"That is all well and good, but you might want to let me take a wee bath first."

They laughed, and joy surged through her from head to toe like a wave of glory, causing the mantle of sorrow and fear she'd carried for what seemed like an eternity to drop from her like a cloak. Beside them, Margaret and Harry were enjoying their own reunion, and she felt another stab of rapture when she heard the peal of her cousin's laughter. All was right in the world.

The two couples walked up the road, arms around each other, heads close together. "I have plans for us, Isabelle. I hope you will approve of them."

A tiny cloud appeared in her sunlit happiness. Did Rory understand that she had been forced from Edinburgh permanently, that his own home was forfeited to the English?

"I know what you are thinking." His eyes were grave. "I know what has happened. I want to take you to America, to the colony of North Carolina. They say the hills are almost as beautiful as ours."

A vision of distant, lovely hills drifted into Isabelle's mind like a dream. Hills where they could build a life together, free from persecution and fear. Maybe she would even discover new healing plants there in the meadows and woods. She took his hand and squeezed.

"Oh yes, Rory, I will go. Wherever you are is my home."

20

Creighton, Vermont
Present Day

Marla knelt beside Wendell on the ballroom floor, an expression of helplessness and fear on her face. "Someone please help him!"

"What happened?" Sofia asked, hunkering down beside her friend.

Before Marla could answer, a man shouldered his way through the bystanders. "Let me through. I'm a doctor."

"Stand back, everyone," Jim said, waving his arms. "Give him room." Sofia saw familiar faces in the circle. Laura rushed forward, but Sandy grabbed her arm to halt her.

"He collapsed while we were dancing." Marla had a note of panic in her voice, and Sofia put a comforting arm around her.

The doctor crouched next to Wendell and quickly checked his vital signs. "Call an ambulance," he commanded.

"Already done," Jim said.

"The firehouse is nearby. It'll only be a few minutes," someone in the rear of the crowd said.

"What's wrong with him, doctor?" Sofia asked, her arm still around Marla's shoulders. She knew the situation was especially troubling to the widow, as she had already experienced a traumatic loss once.

He shook his head. "I'm not sure. We've got to get him to the hospital, stat." He proceeded to loosen Wendell's collar and remove his bulky belt and sporran, which he handed to Marla. "He won't need these for now."

"I think his wallet is in here," Marla said, giving the sporran to Sofia. "Can you pull it out? The hospital will need his ID."

The fur pouch felt silky under Sofia's fingers, speaking to its quality. She unbuttoned it and peered inside. A wallet and car keys and a comb. And something else—the bottle of supplements she had seen in his booth. A terrible thought flashed across her mind. She had come to fear that Madelaine was poisoned. *Was Wendell also a victim?*

Standing up, she gestured for the doctor to step away from the group. Then she handed him the bottle. "You'd better have these tested."

The double doors to the ballroom burst open and two EMTs ran in with a gurney. Jim waved them over to Wendell.

The doctor took the bottle and studied it, his eyes narrowing with suspicion. "What do you mean?"

"They may have been tampered with. Trust me."

"If you know something—" His tone was almost threatening.

"I don't, for sure. But I'd be happy to talk to the police."

He shook the bottle of pills. "If there is anything here, you'll be their first call."

"Fine." Sofia turned, searching for Jim and her friends. The crowd had thinned out, most people obviously feeling the party was over. Laura and Sandy were among those who left.

Sofia yawned as she unlocked the food truck early the next morning, wishing she could have stayed in bed a few more hours. It had been a long night. They had stayed at the hospital until they got the good news that Wendell was going to pull through. Thanks to her finding the pills, the doctors had been able to identify a suitable treatment and antidote. Once the police had arrived, Sofia had to explain more than once—backed up by her friends—about Madelaine's mysterious symptoms. They'd taken Madelaine's pills away for analysis too.

She pulled the door open and stepped inside. At first she wasn't sure what she was seeing. Then it sank in. The inside of the truck was trashed.

Baking pans and utensils littered the floor and countertops. Jagged blue shards announced the demise of her favorite mixing bowl. Even the broom closet was empty, the mop and broom lying across the narrow space in an *X*. The dustpan rested atop the stove.

Worst of all, a coating of flour lay over everything, like ash from an explosion.

Sofia's eyes went from disaster to disaster, her mind spinning in disbelief, unable to order her thoughts. *Where do I begin?*

She bent to pick up a bottle of expensive real vanilla, which fortunately was intact.

"Oh my, what happened here?" Laura stood in the doorway, eyes wide behind her glasses.

Sofia set the bottle down with shaking fingers. "Someone broke in." She could barely speak, the sense of violation was so strong.

Laura edged inside, her foot striking an empty soda can from the overturned recycle bin. The light metal bounced across the floor with a clatter.

Kick the can. Sofia shook her head at this nonsensical thought. She'd never be able to get the place cleaned up in time to bake for the day. And what about her ingredients for the bake-off? She crunched across the floor to the cabinet to check.

"You already took them out of here, didn't you?" Laura's tone held a menacing edge. "Where are they?"

Sofia froze in the act of opening the cabinet door. "Took what?" She was playing dumb, but she knew exactly what Laura was talking about. The herbal supplements.

A crunching sound announced that Laura was walking toward her. "You know what I'm talking about. I saw you give Wendell's herbs to the doctor."

Sofia shut the door, turned, and leaned back against the cabinet, arms crossed in an attempt to appear unconcerned. She shrugged. "I thought he might have had a reaction to something. That's all."

Laura stepped closer. Her round cheeks shone bright red and sweat gleamed on her forehead. "I don't believe you." Her gray eyes were like lasers.

Sofia's heart kicked into gear as adrenaline surged, much like the time she had come face-to-face with a black bear on a hiking trail. She sensed Laura was now equally savage and unpredictable. With an enormous effort, she tried to speak in a calming tone. *Soothe the savage beast.* "It's true. Ask him if you want." To her own ears, she sounded shaky and terrified.

Laura's arm was a blur as she slashed at Sofia. Sofia twisted away just in time.

Laura clutched a metal spindle in her fist. Sofia barely registered it before Laura came at her again. Sofia held up a baking pan to fend off the blow. "It's too late, Laura. The police know about Wendell, and Madelaine too."

Laura paused for a few seconds, panting. "You figured out I added a little something extra to Madelaine's supplements." Her laugh was eerie. "What a nerve she had, confiding in me about her feelings for Wendell. As if I would want to help her."

"That must have been terrible," Sofia said, injecting a false note of sympathy into her voice. Meanwhile, she frantically scanned the area for a weapon of her own.

Laura stepped closer, forcing Sofia back against the wall.

"She knew I was in love with him. For years and years. He was supposed to be mine after he left Sandy."

"So you decided they both needed to die." Sofia spotted something out of the corner of her eye. Could she reach it in time? She sidled sideways closer to the counter. "Killing me won't avenge you."

"But it will feel good." With a roar, Laura launched herself at Sofia, her arm a blur as she jabbed again and again.

Sofia blocked her with a knee as she groped for the one item that could help. Not a knife, unfortunately, as those were on the floor somewhere.

Annie's rolling pin. Twenty inches of marble, perfect for piecrust, shortbread, and self-defense.

Without thought, she grabbed it and hit Laura on the side of her head.

Laura's knees sagged, and she collapsed to the floor. Sofia quickly grabbed the deadly spindle from her hand. "No, Wynter will not be taking any more lessons from you," she said.

"Och, what's all this?" Annie stood in the doorway, her bright eyes taking in every detail of the scene. She fumbled for her phone in her apron pocket. "I think I'd better call the police for ye."

Sofia put a hand over her face. "Please do." Gathering her wits, she stepped over Laura and exited the truck. She'd lock her in until help arrived.

Sofia took several steadying breaths and wiped her hands on her apron, her gaze skimming the ingredients lined up on the countertop for the bake-off. *I have everything, right? I remember how to cook, don't I?*

After Laura was arrested and Sofia spent the day being questioned by the police, it had been a real crunch preparing for the final phase of the contest. Fortunately, Annie came to the rescue and provided all the ingredients Sofia needed at her own expense. "The least I could do for ye, lass," she said. "One good turn deserves another. Go on, make me proud."

She took a deep breath, praying she could justify Annie's faith in her baking ability. Everyone else's faith too, as a matter of fact.

Her family and friends sat in the audience just outside the circle of lights, she knew, but the bright spotlights prevented her from seeing their smiling faces. The bake-off was being filmed for use in Best Biscuits commercials and promotions. The enormous fairgrounds kitchen and dining facility were decorated for the occasion with Best Biscuits banners and props.

"All right, people," the director said in his booming voice. "Are we ready?"

Sofia nodded, as did Sandy, who stood at an adjacent counter. *She looks scared too.*

The director gave the signal, and they were off in a flurry of preparations. Both Sofia and Sandy used recipes that called for refrigerated dough, so they took a break while the dough firmed up.

Sofia rested in the small office serving as her greenroom. Closing her eyes, she put her head down on the desk. *It will be okay if I don't win. It's an honor to get this far. The notoriety will be good for my business too.*

Her reassurances didn't really ring true, but they helped prevent her from screaming with impatience. Never again. Her nerves couldn't take it.

"Sofia?"

She glanced up from her musings to see Dr. Campbell, the expert on Scottish history.

He stepped into the room, waving papers in one hand. "Sorry to bother you, but they said you were on break."

"It's fine, really. Maybe you can take my mind off the contest for a minute."

"I understand. It's tough waiting." He pulled up a chair and sat heavily. "I found something, you see, about your Isabelle Ripa."

All thoughts of the contest mercifully fled. "Really? Tell me."

"I was most fortunate to stumble across this. Awhile ago I bought a collection of eighteenth- and nineteenth-century diaries. Among them was one by Margaret MacDonald Campbell." Forestalling her question, he added, "She was Isabelle's cousin, perhaps married to an ancestor of mine."

"That is amazing." Sofia caught her breath in excitement.

"It's always a thrill to ferret out knowledge about one's forebears." His brows beetled. "Well, almost always. Criminal activity—"

"Isabelle," Sofia prompted.

"Yes. Sorry." He glanced at the paper. "According to the diary, Rory MacGregor fought in the Battle of Culloden, the last stand of Bonnie Prince Charlie's Jacobite Uprising. MacGregor was a brave man and well regarded by all. After the failure of the Jacobite cause, he married Isabelle and they immigrated to North Carolina."

"How romantic." So the square was indeed from Rory MacGregor's tartan.

"There's more, and this is the really incredible part. Margaret goes on to say Isabelle was an herbalist, and this knowledge helped her solve 'murder most foul'—the death of a Lord Lochmere in Edinburgh. Apparently she received a sizable reward for doing so." He laughed. "Can you believe that she solved a murder?"

"Yes, actually I can. It runs in the family." The buzzer sounded and Sofia stood. "I've got to go. Thanks again, Dr. Campbell." As she swept from the room, she suppressed a smile at the historian's puzzled expression.

Spirits buoyed by the information about Isabelle, Sofia performed her next tasks with great efficiency and flair. The cookie dough seemed to cooperate too. It rolled out to the correct thickness without sticking, and each Scottie dog was perfect.

She didn't spare a glance for Sandy but sensed the woman was working just as hard on her batch. The oven timers even went off within seconds of each other. Holding her breath, Sofia opened the door and pulled out her baking sheet with mitt-clad hands. Each cookie was lightly and evenly browned.

She had never baked such beautiful cookies. She hoped they tasted as good as they looked. Carefully wielding the spatula, she moved the shortbread to the racks to cool. In addition to Barclay Best and Donna Roberts, other high-ranking officials from Best Biscuits were judging. They moved along in single file to get their first look at the completed cookies.

"Aren't they beautiful?" Donna cooed, waving for the cameraman to get close-ups of the golden cookies sitting in tidy rows on the racks.

Sofia studied each face, hoping to glean clues as to their approval or distaste, but they all kept their faces carefully neutral. She thought she saw a raised brow or two at her Scottie dogs. It certainly made her cookies stand out.

When the judges returned to their seats and it was time to move the cookies to the tasting plates, Sofia slid on gloves and picked up the first cookie.

"Stop that man! Stop him, I say!"

Beyond the lights, Sofia saw figures rising to their feet, voices joining in the commotion. She abandoned her cookies and moved to the edge of the stage so she could see beyond the lights.

Annie was chasing a man in overalls across the room. Vanessa jumped to her feet. "That's the man with the mouse," she said.

Sofia ran to cut off the man's escape through a side door close to her. Jim caught on and joined in the pursuit. The foursome crashed into one another at the door, Jim managing to position himself so the man couldn't leave.

"Let me go. I haven't done anything!" the man exclaimed.

"Then you can hold your horses," Annie said.

By now the entire room was in pandemonium as everyone began to babble about the strange turn of events.

Donna clattered across the floor in her heels. "What's the meaning of this? You're ruining the contest." She glared at each of them in turn.

"We think this man sabotaged the contest by putting a mouse in Annie's truck," Sofia said crisply. "He tried to do the same thing to me, but my daughter thwarted him."

"Is this true?" Donna turned her eagle eye on the man.

"Of course not. I'm a handyman for the fairgrounds."

"What's your name?" Donna asked.

Sylvia, the office manager, came bustling up, peering at the man over her glasses. "Harvey Wallace. He is a handyman. I hired him myself." Her mouth set in a grim line. "He's Sandy Wallace's cousin."

The audience erupted in roars of disbelief and excitement. The judges conferred. Security finally arrived and escorted Harvey to the office for further questioning. As Sofia retreated to her station, she wondered what would happen to the contest now.

Finally Donna moved to the front of the room, signaling that a decision had been reached. "We're going to clear the room, folks. The contest appears to have been tainted."

Everyone groaned and Sofia's heart sank. Had she come this far only to have the contest fall apart at the last moment? Then determination flooded her. Perhaps she couldn't change their decision, but she could try.

Not giving herself time to change her mind, she moved to the center of the room beside Donna. "I have something to say."

Donna turned a beady glare on her, and Sofia knew she was going to refuse.

But before Donna could respond, the crowd began to call out.

"Come on!"

"Let her talk!"

"It's only fair!"

Finally, the other woman conceded. "All right. Go ahead."

"I think we should complete the contest. After all, we don't know if Sandy had anything to do with Harvey's actions, right? I know I've worked really hard—we both have—and I think it's only fair that the judges taste our cookies."

People cheered, but Sofia held up her hand to indicate she wasn't finished. "You can decide what to do with the results later. If Sandy wins, wait until the situation is resolved. And if I do—well, it's all good, right?"

She reached out, grabbed one of Sandy's cookies, and took a big bite. "Wow. This is fantastic." She smiled at Sandy. "Can I have your recipe?"

"No," was Sandy's quick reply, sweetened by a grateful smile.

Everyone burst into laughter and applause. "All right, everyone," Donna said after the noise died down. "I guess we're outvoted here. Let the judging begin."

Sofia and Sandy finished moving their cookies to serving plates, and the judging began. Sofia was glad to see that the judges seemed to be according Sandy's cookies the same careful treatment as they had her own. Even if Sandy was guilty, Sofia wanted to win the contest on her own merit.

Sofia felt ready to scream by the time the judges came to their decision. *At least no one could accuse them of being hasty.* When Donna stepped forward, a deep hush fell over the room.

"Thank you all for your patience. This was not an easy decision."

"No kidding," some joker called out.

Donna gave a weak smile and continued. "That is why we will be giving both bakers a contract with Best Biscuits." She waved toward Sofia. "However, Sofia Parker, of Sofia's Confectionery, is the grand-prize winner."

The room exploded with cheers, accompanied by much stamping of feet and hoots and whistles.

Joy suffused Sofia, and for a moment she felt dizzy. She'd done it. She'd won the contest fair and square. Visions of her cookies on shelves all across the country flashed in her head.

Wynter and Vanessa ran forward to hug Sofia, followed by Jim and the boys.

"And," Donna continued when the cheering died down, "Sandy Wallace, of Wallace Treats, is the second-place winner and will receive a conditional contract based on the outcome of the investigation."

Sofia disentangled herself from her excited family and strode over to Sandy's station, her hand outthrust. "Congratulations."

Sandy's hand was limp in hers. She gave Sofia a halfhearted smile. "Thanks. It's better than nothing, I suppose."

Gracious in victory. Not. Sofia felt her own smile harden, and she stepped away without another word. If it hadn't been for her intervention, Sandy would be facing nothing but disgrace.

"Congratulations, honey." Bill, the food inspector, appeared and gave Sandy a hug and kiss on the cheek.

The last piece of the puzzle fell into place for Sofia. The disqualification attempts were orchestrated, with Bill showing up to inspect right after Harvey planted a rodent. She knew without needing to await the outcome of the investigation that Sandy would see nothing from the contest at all.

Shaking her head, she returned her attention to her family.

"Can I have a cookie, Mom?" Matthew's hand hovered over the racks where the leftover cookies sat.

"Go ahead. But only one. Otherwise you'll spoil your dinner."

Matthew and the other kids descended on the treats. Jim put his arm around Sofia. "I'm so proud of you."

"I couldn't have done it without you." She kissed him on the cheek. "Behind every great woman . . ." They grinned at each other.

Donna bustled up, a sheaf of papers in her hand. "Congratulations, Sofia. I've got some paperwork for you to fill out regarding our agreement with you to use your recipe." She glanced at the munching children. "From now on, you can't use that recipe in any other commercial activities. I want to make sure you're good with that."

"Of course." She'd create new ones. She reached for the paperwork, but Jim got there first.

"Thanks. We'll have our attorney review the agreement." He nodded firmly at Donna, whose mouth dropped in surprise.

Sofia was as surprised as Donna but thankful for Jim's intervention. He was right, though. She needed to thoroughly understand the contract before signing. "We'll get back to you as soon as possible," she said.

After Donna clicked away on her high heels, Jim turned to Sofia. "Ready to go home, Mrs. Parker?"

Matthew tugged on Sofia's sleeve, cookie crumbs still lingering in the corners of his mouth. "I can't wait to show Fergus his new house. Think he'll like it?"

Sofia handed him a napkin. "I'm sure he will. Tell the others we're getting ready to go." Matthew wiped his mouth, gave his mother the used napkin, and ran off. Then she remembered something. "We still have to pack up the food truck and the cabin."

"All taken care of," Jim whispered in her ear. "The kids planned a party for you at home with Marla and Julie's help. So get ready to put on your surprised face."

"Thanks for the warning, honey." She put her arm through his. "Let's go home."